Leo pushed hims[elf] [from the] doorframe and tu[rned to look at] her. "You should loosen up," he threw over his shoulder. "You might find that life's less hard work when you're not continually arguing the finer points. You might actually *enjoy* being subservient."

Heather was transfixed by the sight of him, and by the sound of his murmured, lazy voice. It was like a drug, making her thoughts sluggish and not giving her time to get herself all worked up by what he was saying.

"Subservient? I—I can't think of anything worse...." she stammered.

"No? Funny. Every woman I have ever known has ended up enjoying being controlled... not in the boardroom, of course."

He was standing right in front of her and Heather took a couple of little steps back.

"Good for them."

"You are not like them, however. That much I'll concede. But I guarantee there's one order I can give you that you'll jump to obey."

"What?" she challenged, her nerves skittering as he produced a wicked grin.

"Leave now or else watch me undress."

CATHY WILLIAMS was born in the West Indies and has been writing Harlequin® romances for more than fifteen years. She is a great believer in the power of perseverance as she had never written anything before (apart from school essays a lifetime ago!), and from the starting point of zero has now fulfilled her ambition to pursue this most enjoyable of careers. She would encourage any would-be writer to have faith and go for it!

She lives in the beautiful Warwickshire countryside with her husband and three children, Charlotte, Olivia and Emma. When not writing she is hard-pressed to find a moment's free time between the millions of household chores, not to mention being a one-woman taxi service for her daughters' never-ending social lives. She derives inspiration from the hot, lazy, tropical island of Trinidad (where she was born), from the peaceful countryside of middle England and, of course, from her many friends, who are a rich source of plots and are particularly garrulous when it comes to describing Harlequin Presents heroes. It would seem, from their complaints, that tall, dark and charismatic men are way too few and far between! Her hope is to continue writing romance fiction and providing those eternal tales of love for which, she feels, we all strive.

HIRED FOR THE BOSS'S BEDROOM
CATHY WILLIAMS

~ Her Irresistible Boss ~

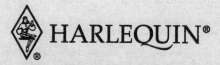

TORONTO • NEW YORK • LONDON
AMSTERDAM • PARIS • SYDNEY • HAMBURG
STOCKHOLM • ATHENS • TOKYO • MILAN • MADRID
PRAGUE • WARSAW • BUDAPEST • AUCKLAND

Recycling programs
for this product may
not exist in your area.

ISBN-13: 978-0-373-52773-1

HIRED FOR THE BOSS'S BEDROOM

First North American Publication 2010.

Copyright © 2009 by Cathy Williams.

For questions and comments about the quality of this book please contact us at Customer_eCare@Harlequin.ca.

® and TM are trademarks of the publisher. Trademarks indicated with ® are registered in the United States Patent and Trademark Office, the Canadian Trade Marks Office and in other countries.

www.eHarlequin.com

Printed in U.S.A.

HIRED FOR THE
BOSS'S BEDROOM

CHAPTER ONE

OF COURSE, Leo had known what his mother was thinking when she had said, without any hint of inflection in her voice, that they had hoped he might have arrived a little earlier—several hours earlier, she could have said, were she to have been absolutely precise. Instead, she had held back her obvious disappointment and had listened to his excuses without comment.

Meetings had overrun. An urgent call had come through just as he had been leaving the office. Inevitable Friday traffic. Leo had kept the excuses brief, knowing that his mother would never actually tell him exactly what she was thinking, would never express disapproval or condemnation. In fact, he doubted whether there had been any need at all to make excuses, but politeness had driven him to apologise just as politeness had driven his mother to respond as she had, without any hint of censure.

'Daniel,' she had said eventually, 'has popped out to see Heather. Just next door. The quickest way is to walk across the fields to her house, but I expect you would rather drive. Or, of course, you could wait here. I told Heather that he was to be back no later than seven.'

'I'll walk.' He would not take the car because, as a city gent, a billionaire who had no time for country walks, he would never choose to wait.

So now here he was, sampling at first hand the extensive acreage that surrounded the exquisite country house which he had bought for his mother over six years ago following his father's death.

Leo had never stepped foot beyond the neatly manicured gardens surrounding the house. Naturally, he had known that the grounds stretched as far as the eye could see, encompassing fields and a thickly wooded area which became lush with lilac lavender during the warm summer-months. Hadn't he, after all, carefully read the reports sent to him by the people he had commissioned to find the property in the first place? Hadn't he duly noted the practicality of his mother living in a house which would not, in due course, find itself surrounded by housing estates due to greedy building contractors having no respect for open space?

But only now, as he tramped across the endless fields, inappropriately clad in handmade leather shoes and a pale-grey suit which had cost the earth, did he appreciate the true size of his investment. Surely his mother, now edging towards her seventies, didn't ever explore the furthest reaches of the estate?

It occurred to him that in truth he had no real inkling as to what his mother did from one day to the next. He dutifully telephoned three times a week—or considerably more now that Daniel had landed on the scene—and was told that she was fine, Daniel was fine, the house was fine, *life* was fine. Then he would attempt to have a conversation with Daniel, which elicited much the same response but in a rather more hostile tone of voice. The details of this *fine* life were never painted in, so he was at a loss to know whether his mother actually realised just how much walking this hike to 'the house next door' entailed.

He cursed himself for thinking that he would enjoy the

fresh air and exercise. Fresh air, he acknowledged—swatting past some brambles, while the summer sunshine reminded him of the folly of venturing out in the countryside wearing a jacket—was best confined to those brief mini-breaks called holidays which he took a couple of times a year—usually combining them with work, women or, more often than not, both. As for exercise, he got ample amounts of that at his London gym where he thrashed out the stress of his high-powered job on a punching bag and then cooled down with fifty-odd laps in the Olympic-sized swimming pool. No one could accuse him of being unfit. This, however, seemed to require a different sort of stamina. He found himself wishing that he had had the foresight to bring his mobile phone with him, because he could have usefully used the time to make a couple of calls, which he would now have to do when he returned to the house.

Heather's house, his mother had assured him, couldn't be missed—it was a small, white, cosy cottage and the garden was spilling over with flowers of every description. Her face had softened when she had said this, and he had wondered whether Heather was one of her pals from the village, someone with whom she shared gossip once a week over pots of tea.

Or something along those lines, at any rate.

It was a heartening thought. Somehow he felt less of the guilty older-son, knowing that his mother had someone virtually on her doorstep with whom she could pass the time of day. And less of the guilty absentee-father, knowing that this kindly neighbour had also bonded with his son.

The cottage in question leapt out at him without warning, and his mother was right; there was no danger of him missing it. 'Strike out west and head for the house that looks as though it belongs in the pages of a fairy tale'. Leo hadn't realised that so many types of flora existed, and he surprised himself by pausing for a couple of seconds to admire the profusion of colour.

Then he circled the cottage, noting the white picket-fence, the clambering roses, all those tell-tale signs of someone who was seriously into clichés. He almost expected to spot a couple of garden gnomes peering out from between the riot of flowers that bordered the little stone path to the front door, but fortunately he was spared that particular horror.

Leo himself was minimalist to the bone. His London penthouse apartment paid homage to the axiom 'less is more': black leather, chrome and glass. On the white walls, outrageously expensive, abstract paintings were splashes of colour that slowly appreciated in value even as they adorned his walls; it was why he had bought them in the first place.

The door knocker appeared to be some quirky, mythical creature. Leo banged on it twice, just in case he was dealing with someone hard of hearing.

He heard the sound of quickly approaching footsteps, and something that sounded like muffled laughter. Then the door was opened and he found himself staring down into the bluest eyes he had ever seen. A tangle of pure gold, curly hair framed a heart-shaped face, and as his eyes involuntarily travelled further downwards they took in the small, curvaceous figure that, in a society that prized the stick-thin figure, would be labelled 'overweight'.

'Who are you?' he demanded without preamble, lounging against the door frame.

'You must be Daniel's dad.' Heather stood aside to let him enter. She couldn't help herself. Disapproval had seeped into her voice, and he must have noticed it, because his ebony brows pleated into a frown.

'And you must be Heather. I was expecting someone… older.'

Heather could have told him that he was exactly what *she* had been expecting. Her neighbour Katherine had talked about him, of course, had told her all about his meteoric career in the city. And Heather had heard between the lines a description of a workaholic, someone who was driven to succeed, someone who had precious little time for the things that mattered most in life. A lousy son and an even lousier father.

Up close and personal, he was every inch the successful businessman she had expected.

He was also incredibly good-looking; this bit was doing its best to nudge a hole in her disapproval. A lot better looking than those grainy pictures she had been shown in the scrap book Katherine kept of all his achievements, in fact. Indeed, the man was drop-dead gorgeous. Raven-black hair framed a face whose perfect, chiselled symmetry was harshly, coolly sensational. His eyes were grey and watchful, eyes that chose to give nothing away. She felt a shockingly potent quiver of awareness, then thankfully the moment was gone, lost under the weight of her disapproval.

Charitable by nature, Heather knew that it was crazy to judge a book by its cover, but she had had more than a passing brush with arrogance and success. Some women might find all that power and wealth an incredible turn on, but she knew from first-hand experience the price that had to be paid for being attracted to such dazzling light: too high.

'I have come for my son.' Having cursorily inspected the tiny hall, with its cosy flag-stoned floor and bowls of flowers on the window ledges by the door, Leo swung back round to face the woman who appeared to be dithering by the front door.

It had been a hot day, and she was wearing what looked

like a loose, flowing gypsy-style affair, the sort of outfit that had been fashionable once upon a time. She was also looking at him with the sort of expression that promised a lecture, given half a chance. Leo sincerely hoped she would keep whatever was on her mind to herself, and he had an inkling of an idea what it was. He had no time for lectures, well-intentioned or otherwise.

'He's just finishing his tea.'

'His *tea*?'

'Dinner, if you prefer.'

'Why is he eating here? I told my mother that I would take them both out for something to eat.'

'I guess he just got hungry.' Heather refrained from adding to that statement. The fact was, Daniel had refused point-blank to have dinner with his father.

'Well, thank you very much, but it might have been worth finding out first whether plans had been made.'

This was just too much. Heather slipped past Leo to the kitchen, where she told Daniel that his father was here, and registered his expression of scowling indifference. Then she quietly shut the kitchen door and folded her arms.

'On the subject of *plans*…' she delivered coldly, ignoring the forbidding expression on his face.

'Before you go any further, I'm in no mood to listen to someone I don't know from Adam climbing on a podium and giving me a lecture.'

Faced with such a blunt, arrogant dismissal of what she had been about to say, Heather's mouth dropped open, and Leo took that as immediate and obedient closure on a subject about which he had little interest. He walked past her towards the kitchen but she caught his wrist. It was like being zapped with a very powerful electric charge, and it took all her will power to stand her ground and not cower. She suspected that this was a man who specialised in inspiring fear.

'I think we should talk before you get your son, Mr West.'

'The name's Leo; I think we can dispense with the formalities, considering you're apparently an honorary member of the family.' He looked at her small hand circling his wrist and then back to her face. 'And I guarantee that whatever you have to say is going to be of little interest to me. So why not spare yourself the sermon?'

'I don't intend to give you a sermon.'

'Wonderful! Then what exactly is it you want to talk about?' He glanced at his watch. 'But you'll have to make it short, I'm afraid. It's been a hellish trip up here, and I have work to do when I get back to the house.'

Heather took a deep breath. 'Okay. I *am* a little annoyed.'

Leo made no effort to conceal his impatience. In that rarefied world in which he lived, people didn't get *annoyed* with him—least of all women—but this one was practically pulsating, so he shrugged. He would let her have her say, and then he would clear off with his son. 'Okay. Spit it out.'

'In the sitting room. I don't want Daniel to hear us.'

She led the way, acutely conscious of him behind her. Once they were both in the room, staring at each other like combatants in an arena, she said in a controlled voice, 'I don't think you realise how disappointed Daniel was that you didn't make it to his Sports Day. It's a big deal at the school, and he'd been practising for weeks.'

Leo flushed guiltily. Of course he had known that this would be flung at him but it still irked him, that this perfect stranger had the brazenness to stand there, staring at him with wide, accusing, critical eyes.

'That, as I explained to my mother, was unavoidable—

and, now you've got that off your chest, I think I'll leave with my son.'

'Why was it unavoidable?' Heather persisted. 'Don't tell me that there was something more important than seeing your son come first in the hundred-metre sprint?'

'Actually, I don't have to tell you anything,' Leo informed her coolly. 'I don't make a habit of explaining myself to anyone, least of all someone I've known for—what?—roughly fifteen minutes. I don't recall my mother even mentioning your name in any of the conversations I've had with her.'

That came as no surprise to Heather. Daniel went to the local private school. He stayed in the house with Katherine, and occasionally, over the past eight months his father had deigned to visit, usually on a Sunday; a full weekend presumably was just too much for him. More often than not, he imported both Katherine and Daniel to London, sending his driver to collect them on the Saturday morning, and delivering them back to the country promptly on the Sunday afternoon.

Anyone would think that a man who had lost his son for years, when his ex-wife had disappeared off to Australia, would have wanted to spend as much time as possible making up for the wasted time!

Clearly not the man standing in front of her.

Katherine would not have mentioned Heather because her son would have had zero interest in finding out about the people who figured in his mother's life. From what Heather had gleaned, Leo West was an utterly selfish money-making machine.

'I realise I don't have any right to tell you how to lead your life,' Heather said, doing her best to be fair, 'but Daniel needs you. He would never say so because he's probably scared of you.'

'Has he told you that he's scared of me?' This conversation was now becoming bizarre. He had expected to be greeted by a motherly lady, maybe to be offered a cup of tea, which he would, naturally, have refused; to leave with his son in tow, any sullenness over his absence at the wretched Sports Day to be forgotten when he presented him with the present he had bought. It was the very latest mobile phone, capable of doing pretty much anything bar washing the dishes and cooking the meals.

Instead, he was being held to account by a twenty-something girl with a challenged sense of dress who had probably never set foot out of the village.

'He doesn't have to. I can tell. He doesn't see enough of you. I know it's none of my business, but relationships have to be worked on. Daniel's a very vulnerable little boy, and he needs his father. Especially now. He's suffered the loss of his mother. He needs the security of his dad to see him through.'

'You're right—it's none of your business.'

'You're not much into listening to what other people have to say, are you?' Heather flared angrily.

'On the contrary, I spend a good deal of my time listening to what other people have to say. I just have no interest in an interfering neighbour regaling me with amateur psychobabble—unless, of course, you have some kind of degree in child psychology. Do you?'

'No, I don't, but—'

'Well, maybe you're his teacher, hmm…?'

'No, I'm not. But that's not the—'

'And you're not exactly a lifelong friend of my mother's, are you? I'm sure, if you were, I might just have a passing idea of who you are.'

'No, but—'

'In fact, when and how did you exactly come into contact with my mother?'

'We met a while back, at a gardening convention at the

village hall. A television celebrity was giving a talk about orchids, and we both just—'

'Fascinating, but here's what I'm wondering—what's a young girl like you doing at *gardening conventions*? Isn't that the luxury of retired people who have endless time on their hands to potter around in their gardens? Don't you have more exciting things to do? You know, if you did, maybe you wouldn't find yourself drawn to nosing into other people's lives.'

Leo was in equal measure outraged that she'd dared to voice opinions that breached his personal boundaries, and borderline distracted by the rising tide of colour that was colouring her cheeks. The woman blushed like a virgin, and it struck him that he wasn't very often in the company of a woman whose face was so transparent. He favoured the career woman, and it had to be said that career women weren't given to blushing.

'How *dare* you?'

'Pretty easily, as a matter of fact,' Leo commented smoothly. 'Don't go on the attack unless you're ready for a fight—first law of success.'

Heather looked at the impossibly handsome man staring coolly at her, and wanted to fly across the room and punch him in his arrogant face. That reaction was so out of character for her that she closed her eyes briefly and blinked it away. She was placid by nature, not given to screeching hysterics. So who was this wild creature that had taken over her body?

'Okay,' she said tightly. 'You're right. Your relationship with your son is no business of mine. I'll go and get him right now.' She walked towards the door and only looked at him to say quietly, 'And, for your information, I have a job and I don't *nose* into other people's private lives because I have nothing better to do with my life. I wanted to be helpful. I'm very sorry you misread my intentions.'

Instead of feeling like the victor in what had always promised to be a pointless exchange from where he was standing, Leo now felt like the villain. How had that happened? He had said what needed to be said, had told her to keep out of his business, she had agreed—so why did he now feel as though he had won the battle but lost the war?

Always the winner in any verbal showdown, Leo was unaccustomed to being caught on the back foot, and for the first time he was rendered temporarily speechless. He found that he was staring into space and hurried out, almost bumping into Daniel, who greeted him with a sulky glower.

'I… I apologise for missing your Sports Day, Daniel,' Leo began, very much aware of Heather standing in the background—probably committing this awkward little scene to memory so that she could bring it out at a later date and use it against him should the opportunity ever again arise.

'Whatever.'

'I hear you came first in the hundred-metre sprint,' Leo said, trying to bring the tension down a notch or two. 'Well done!'

He looked at Heather, and as their eyes tangled she felt a wave of sympathy for the man. Of course, he didn't deserve her sympathy. From all accounts, he threw money at his son but rarely gave him the time that was so essential. But, her naturally warm nature reluctantly seeing the situation from both points of view, how hard it must be, she thought, for him to incorporate a young child into his life? Up until eight months ago, he had been completely unaware of his son's existence, and had been accustomed to doing everything his own way, with no need to consider the welfare of another human being.

'He's a star,' she interjected into the silence, moving forward and pulling Daniel towards her in a natural embrace. She wondered how his father couldn't be charmed by his gorgeous, dark-haired seven-year-old son with those big brown eyes and skinny, vulnerable legs sticking out from his school shorts, which he had yet to change out of. 'Aren't you, Dan?' She ruffled his hair affectionately and then said brightly, 'You have a wonderful weekend, and don't forget you can pop over any time if you want help with your English homework!'

Relegated to the sidelines, Leo saw that rarest of things, a shy smile of warmth and affection from his son. Naturally not directed at *him*, but a smile nevertheless. He looked at his watch and said briskly, 'I think we should be heading back to the house now, Daniel; leave Heather to get on with…whatever she has to get on with.'

'Can't you come across on the weekend?' Daniel suddenly turned to Heather with a pleading look, which of course immediately made Leo frown impatiently. Was his own company so dire that his son needed rescuing from any possibility of prolonged, unwanted bonding at all costs? Leo was uncomfortably reminded of Heather's little talk, the first little talk he had had on the subject of his son since he had met him on that plane at Heathrow all those months ago.

'We could go see that Disney movie,' Daniel was now saying with a touch of desperation in his voice. 'You know, you told me that you wanted to see it but you would have to rent a child to take along…'

'I'm sorry, Daniel. I've got heaps of things to do, and I was just teasing when I said that I wanted to see that movie. I don't actually *like* Disney movies.'

'You've got lots of them in that cabinet in your sitting room,' Daniel was quick to point out, with the unerring talent of a child to say precisely the wrong thing at the wrong time.

Heather reddened, cleared her throat, could think of nothing to say, reddened a bit more and eventually broke the expectant silence. 'I'll think about it.'

Of course, she had no intention of going to a movie with them, or going anywhere else for that matter.

She had spoken her mind, for better or for worse, and had met with a resounding lack of success. Leo West was egotistical, driven to the point of obsession and would never take advice from anyone, least of all from a woman like her. Hadn't he assumed that she busied herself meddling in other people's lives because she had no life of her own?

She had a life. A very good one!

In the stillness of the cottage, which seemed unnaturally quiet when her warring visitors had disappeared, she considered the excellent life she had.

Wonderful job, doing the one thing she couldn't have been happier doing, illustrating children's books, getting inspiration from her garden which she translated into pictures that were slowly achieving notoriety as works of art in themselves. She worked from home, travelling into London once a month so that she could go through her graphics with her art editor. It was a real luxury.

She also owned her cottage outright. No mortgage; no debt owing, in fact, to anyone. Which made her as free as a bird.

True, there was no man in her life, but that, she told herself, was exactly how she wanted it.

Little snippets of her past intruded into her peaceful cottage: Brian, as she had first known him when she had still been a young girl of eighteen and he had been on the brink of his glittering career. Blonde hair, straight, thick and always falling across his face, until he had had it cut because, he had told her seriously, in his profession men all wore their hair short.

Heather blinked and shoved that little nest of bitter memories back into their Pandora's box. She had learnt years ago that dwelling on things that couldn't be changed was a waste of time.

Instead, she shifted her attention to the kitchen which still bore the remnants of Daniel's hastily eaten meal of spaghetti Bolognese. His father, he had told her, had planned on taking them out to dinner but he hadn't wanted to go. He hated those fancy restaurants they went to. He hated the food. As a postscript, he had added that he hated his father.

Which made her start thinking of Leo and, once she started, she found that she couldn't seem to stop. That cold, ruthless face swam into her head until she was forced to retreat to her little office and try and lose herself in the illustration she was currently working on. She was peering at the detail of a fairy wing, every pore in her being focused on the minute detail of painting, when the bang on her front door sent her jerking back, knocking over the jar of water, which shattered into a thousand pieces on the wooden floor.

A second bang, more demanding this time, had her running to the front door before she had time to clean up the slowly spreading mess on the ground.

She pulled open the door before a third bang brought down the roof.

'*You!* What are you doing here?' He was no longer in his suit. Instead, he was wearing a pair of cream trousers and a navy-blue polo shirt. Behind him was a gleaming silver Bentley.

At nearly nine in the evening, the sun had faded to a dull, mellow, grey light.

Leo dealt Heather a grim nod. 'Believe me, I don't want to be here any more than you want me to be here, but I have been put in the difficult position of having to ask you to accompany us to the cinema tomorrow. Daniel has dug his heels in and refused to budge. I'm being blackmailed by someone who hasn't even graduated to books without pictures. It's ridiculous, but it's true, hence the reason I'm here when I should be reading over a due-diligence report that can't wait.'

'I don't know what you're talking about.'

'Why don't you let me in and I can explain?'

'I'm sorry, but can't this wait until tomorrow? It's late, and I have stuff to do.'

'Late?' Leo made a show of consulting his watch. 'It's ten past nine. On a Friday night. Since when is that *late*?'

Heather heard the amused incredulity in his voice and felt her hackles rise.

'I was *working*,' she said stiffly.

'Of course. You never got around to telling me exactly what you do for a living.'

'You aren't interested in what I do for a living.'

Leo thought that she was spot on with that, but circumstances had forced his hand. He had returned to the house with Daniel in frozen silence and had endured what could only be called silent warfare.

The mobile phone had been looked at and then refused, on the grounds of, 'Thank you very much, but the teacher doesn't allow mobile phones at school.'

And, 'It's a kind thought, but young children don't need mobile telephones,' from his mother.

Frustration had almost driven him to ask his mother what the hell was going on because surely, *surely*, this complete lack of co operation couldn't just be caused by the fact that he had missed a Sports Day! But Katherine had taken herself off to bed at a ridiculously early hour, and so here he was, compelled to try and do a patch-up job with the amateur psychologist in the hope that the weekend might not end up a complete write-off.

'You seem to have something on your face…' He rubbed his finger along the blue streak adorning her chin and gazed in bemusement at his finger. 'What is it? Paint? Is that how you spend your Friday evenings—painting your house?'

Heather pushed the door, but Leo wasn't having any of that. He wedged his foot neatly into the open space and met her hostile stare with a grimly determined expression.

'You can't just come here and disturb me at this hour,' she said through gritted teeth.

'Needs must. Now, are you going to let me in?' He stood back and raked his hands impatiently through his hair. 'I don't suppose,' he said heavily, 'that I was the only father who didn't make it to the Sports Day.' It was a concession of sorts and as close to an olive branch that Leo was going to offer.

Situation defused.

'Yes.'

'You're kidding, right?'

'No, I'm not. Every single parent was there, taking pictures. Daniel had asked me to come along to watch, pretended that he didn't care whether you came or not, but I watched him, and he kept looking around for you, wondering if you were somewhere in the crowd.'

'Are you going to let me in?' Leo asked brusquely, not liking this image of himself as some kind of heartless monster.

Heather reluctantly opened the door and allowed him to stride past her. She hadn't noticed earlier, but he dominated the space—not just because he was tall, but because of that aura he exuded, an aura of supreme power. He owned the air around him in a way that Brian never had, even though it had seemed so at the time. She shivered.

'So, where were you painting?' Leo asked, looking around him. He had quizzed his mother about Heather, ignoring her look of surprise at his interest, and had gleaned that she and Daniel trotted over to the cottage whenever they had a chance. Heather had, it would seem, become quite a fixture in the household. Little wonder that she had been polishing her soapbox in anticipation of his arrival.

He followed her into a room at the back of the house, and was confronted by walls on which hung every manner of artwork. Yet more were housed in an antique architect's chest against the wall.

'I broke my glass,' Heather said, kneeling down so that she could begin carefully picking up the shards. 'When you banged on the door. I wasn't expecting anyone.'

'You…paint?'

Heather looked briefly at him and blushed, suddenly feeling vulnerable as those flint-grey eyes roved over the artwork on her walls. 'I told you that I had a job,' she said, before resuming her glass-collecting task. It would take a heck of a lot more elbow grease to fully clean the ground, but the biggest bits had been collected; the elbow grease would have to wait until the morning, because right now she was finding it hard to think properly. She just wanted him out of her cottage so that she could get her scattered wits back into order.

Leo dragged his eyes away from the paintings and focused entirely on the woman standing in front of him. When she had told him that she had a job, he had assumed something along the lines of a secretary, maybe a receptionist somewhere, perhaps. But she was an artist, and it explained a lot. Her apparent lack of any recognisable fashion sense, her woolly-headed assumption that she could say whatever she wanted to say without thinking, her earnest belief that she could somehow solve a situation over a cup of tea and a good chat.

Artists occupied a different world to most normal people. It was common knowledge they lived in a world of their own.

He refocused on the matter at hand. 'I don't know how you've managed to form such a strong bond with my son,' he said, not beating about the bush. 'But after the Sports Day…situation…it seems that the only way this weekend isn't going to descend into a nightmare is if you…' Leo searched around to find the right words. It wasn't in his nature to ask favours of anyone, and having to do so now left a sour taste in his mouth. He especially didn't like asking favours from a woman who got on his nerves. Moreover, he would have to be pleasant towards her.

Leo had tried his damnedest to form a bond with his son, but there was murky water under the bridge, and he had had time to reflect that it wasn't Daniel's fault. Without a great deal of difficulty, he could see any relationship he might have with his son sink without trace beneath a tide of remembered bitterness.

'If I…what?'

'Movies…lunch…dinner. I leave on Sunday afternoon,' he felt compelled to tack on because he could see the dawning dismay spreading across her face.

'You mean you want me to sacrifice my entire weekend to bail you out of a situation you can't handle?'

'*Sacrifice?*' Leo laughed drily. 'I don't think there's a woman alive who has ever seen a weekend spent in my company as a *sacrifice.*'

'That's the problem,' Heather said. 'Men like you never do.'

CHAPTER TWO

Leo decided to leave that half-muttered remark alone. Why get embroiled in a lengthy question-and-answer session with a woman who was an irrelevance in his life? On a more practical note, he needed her for the weekend, because he couldn't face a day and a half of his son's withdrawn sadness. If she could smooth things over, then far be it from him to invite further hostility from her. As far as he was concerned, though, all this interest in a kid who happened to live a couple of fields away from her spoke of an unhealthy lack of social life, but each to their own.

By lunchtime the following day—having spent the morning at the zoo, where his son had displayed an amazing knowledge of animals, rattling off facts to Heather and his mother while studiously ignoring him—Leo was beginning to feel his curiosity piqued.

She exuded warmth, and when she laughed, which she seemed to do often, it was a rich, infectious laughter.

Of course the laughter, like his son's encyclopaedic knowledge of every animal, was not directed at him.

Over a cup of tea in the canteen at the zoo—which Leo could only describe as a marginally more savoury experience than if he had actually pulled his chair into one of the animal enclosures—he noticed that the woman was not strictly limited to conversations about dinosaurs, reptiles and computer games. When his mother asked him about work, in an attempt to include him in the conversation, Leo was taken aback to be quizzed about the politics of mergers and acquisitions in so far as they affected the lives of countless hapless victims of 'marauding conglomerates'.

While his mother tried to hide her amusement, Leo stared at Heather as though she had mutated into one of the animals they had just been feeding.

Marauding conglomerates? Since when did country bumpkins use expressions like that?

He also didn't like the way her mouth curled with scorn when she addressed him, but in front of his mother and Daniel there was nothing he could do but smile coldly at her and change the subject.

Now, with the animals out of the way, he was taking them all to lunch; that nasty little remark she had flung at him the evening before, the remark which he had generously chosen to overlook, was beginning to prey on his mind.

Just who the hell did the woman think she was? Did she imagine that because she was doing him a favour she could indulge in whatever cheap shot she wanted at his expense?

People rarely got under Leo's skin. This particularly applied to women. He was astute when it came to reading their feminine wiles, and could see through any minor sulk to exactly what lay underneath. In short, they were a predictable entity.

As they headed for the Italian on the main street, he stuck his hands in his pockets and murmured, bending so that his words were for her ears only,

'Artist and financial expert, hmm? A woman of many talents. I had no idea you had such a keen interest in the business world.'

Heather pulled back. Something about his warm breath against her face had made the hairs on the back of her neck tingle.

It had been a mistake to let him rattle her, and she had been unable to resist wiping that lazy, condescending expression off his face by parrying with him about finance. Against her will, she had once known those money markets until they were coming out of her ears—and, once learnt, always remembered. It had been worth it just to see the shocked look on his face when she'd thrown in a few technical terms that surely a country hick like her should never have known.

Now, with his gleaming eyes fixed on her, Heather was belatedly realising that she might have been better off keeping her mouth shut and letting him get on with thinking whatever he wanted to think of her.

'I read the newspapers,' she muttered stiffly.

'You'd have to be a very avid reader of the *Financial Times* to know as much as you do about the global trading-market. So what's going on here?'

'Nothing's going on, and can I just remind you that I don't actually have to be here? I only agreed to come because I knew that Daniel would have been disappointed if I hadn't—and he's already had enough disappointment with you missing his Sports Day because of "unavoidable work commitments".'

'It's not going to work, so you can forget it.'

'What's not going to work?'

'Your attempt to change the subject. Who the hell are you *really*? That's the question I can't stop asking myself.'

Ahead of them, Daniel and Katherine were putting a bit of distance between them; when Katherine turned round and gesticulated that she and Daniel were going to pop into his favourite sports shop, Heather could have groaned with despair.

Leo was intrigued by her reaction to his remark. From not

really caring one way or another who she was, he now seriously began to wonder about her provenance.

'Are you always so suspicious?'

'Comes with the territory.'

'And what territory would that be? No, don't bother answering that—I already know.'

'Care to explain?'

'No, not really. If you don't mind, I think I'll just go and see what Katherine and Daniel are up to in there.'

'Oh, I'm sure they won't mind if we go ahead to the restaurant and wait there for them. It's a beautiful day. Why rush?'

'Because I have things to do at the house.'

'What things?'

'None of your business!'

'I'm getting the impression that you don't like me very much. Would I be right in that assumption?' He went into the sports shop to tell his mother that he would wait for them at the restaurant with Heather. No rush; take as long as they wanted. 'But don't buy anything.' He looked at his son, who stared back at him with grudging curiosity. 'I want to see whatever you buy—an athlete like you needs the best equipment.' He was rewarded with something approaching a smile.

The sports shop was an Aladdin's den. Leo reckoned his son could spend a satisfyingly long time browsing with his mother and that, he decided, would give him sufficient time to put his sudden curiosity to bed.

He had no doubt that she would be waiting for him outside. If there was one thing Leo knew with absolute certainty, it was that no one ever walked out on him until he was finished with them.

Sure enough, there she was, peering through the window of the shoe shop, and he took a little time to look at her. The strange gypsy-skirt of the night before had been replaced by something equally shapeless, but it was a hot day and her tee shirt outlined the contours of breasts that would be more than a handful. What would they look like? What would she feel like?

That sudden thought seemed to spring from nowhere and Leo shoved it aside, disconcerted.

The woman was most definitely not his type. After his short-lived and disastrous marriage to Sophia, he had exorcised pretty little airheads from his repertoire of beddable women, and he hadn't looked back.

Although…

The girl next door wasn't exactly quite the airhead he had assumed. Nor was she exactly pretty, although he supposed that there were a fair few men who might look twice at her, with her unruly gold hair and her lush curves.

She turned to find him staring, and he watched that telltale colour bloom into her cheeks.

'They'll be a little while,' Leo said. 'I told them to take their time.'

Heather fell into step with him. Without the presence of Daniel and Katherine, she was suddenly conscious of how intimidating she found him. Even when he was at his most casual, as he was now, in a pair of faded jeans and a white polo-shirt that emphasised his olive complexion.

Five minutes later, which was about long enough for Heather to really feel her nerves go into over drive, they were at the restaurant. It was tucked away up one of the smaller streets in the trendy part of the little town, with wine bars and little boutiques that specialised in selling designer clothes and designer kitchenware. Tables were laid outside, but Leo ignored them, choosing to stroll into the restaurant and net them the quietest table at the very back.

'So,' he said, relaxing his long body into the chair and giving her the benefit of all his undivided attention. 'You never explained your in-depth knowledge of the business markets. And I have to admit I'm curious. Were you a banker before you decided to throw it all aside and devote your life to painting little fairies?'

'I don't paint *little fairies*. I illustrate children's books,' Heather said mutinously. 'And I don't like the way you've manoeuvred me into being here alone with you.'

'Why? You have a suspicious mind. What do you think I'm going to get up to?'

'You have no right to question me about my private life.'

'Of course I have. Until yesterday, I didn't even know you existed. Now I'm to assume that you've become an integral part of my family.'

'I'm not an integral part of your family,' Heather protested. She looked at Leo's dark, clever, shockingly good-looking face with dislike. He was like a shark, patrolling his waters and ready to pounce on anything that might possibly be construed as prey. In this case, her. Wasn't it enough that she was helping him out? Obviously not.

Leo ignored that interruption. Without bothering to glance around, he summoned a waiter, who appeared as if by magic even though the restaurant was busy, and he ordered some wine, his eyes still focused on Heather's face.

'You've known my mother for a year or two, my son for considerably less time, and yet here you are—a vital part of this weekend's activities because you've managed to ingratiate yourself. Furthermore, you dabble in pretty little pictures yet seem to have an astute business mind, and I know when someone's lifting other people's opinions from the business section of a tabloid newspaper. You appear to have some kind of inside knowledge about how stock markets operate. A little unusual for someone who paints fairies, wouldn't you say?'

With a few bits and pieces of information, he had somehow managed to make her sound like a secret-service agent.

'I don't know where you're going with this.'

'Put it this way,' he drawled, taking his time to taste some of the wine that had been brought to their table and keeping those fabulous grey eyes fixed on her. 'In my position, it's always a good idea to be wary of anyone who doesn't fit their brief.'

'And I guess,' she said acidly, 'that my *brief* is the unattractive country girl without a brain cell in her head?'

'Do you think of yourself as unattractive?' Leo pounced on that small, unthinking slip of the tongue, and she flushed with embarrassment.

She could have told him that she never used to. Sure, she had always known that she didn't have the stick-insect glamour of some of the girls she had grown up with, but she had never had an inferiority complex about her looks. Not until she had moved to London with Brian.

However, the last thing Heather intended to do was bare her soul to the man sitting opposite her.

'Do you think I'm after...what? Your mother's money— do you think I might try to con her out of her fortune?'

'Stranger things have been known to happen.' He really couldn't credit that, though. If the woman had a taste for high living, then she was doing a good job of keeping it under wraps. So far he had yet to see her in something that didn't look as though its last home was a charity shop.

Heather didn't say anything. She could have scoffed at his cynicism, but she understood it. Brian had gone from the good-looking boy who had stolen her heart with his floppy blonde hair and sweats to a cold-eyed stranger in expensive clothes. He had made his money and, as the money had rolled in, so too had the gold diggers, the people who'd always been there, wanting something from him.

She sighed and tried to appreciate his suspicions even though they were directed at her.

'I guess so,' she said with a shrug. 'But not in this case. I think your mother's a really sweet lady. We share a passion for plants and flowers, that's all.'

'Is there no one else on whom you could lavish your passion?' Leo asked lazily. 'For all things...horticultural?'

For a second there Heather could feel her skin prickling at what she had imagined he was asking her.

'We get along, and I met Daniel quite by accident. He was exploring the fields; I guess he must have been lonely.' This was the perfect time to turn the tables and do a little accusing of her own, but his presence was stifling, clogging up her brain, turning it to mush. 'Anyway, I think he got lost. I asked him a few questions and he must have felt at ease because he came visiting again; I enjoy having him around.'

'I guess you might,' Leo mused thoughtfully. 'You must get very lonely in that cottage of yours. Working from home is an isolated way of earning an income. I'm surprised someone as young as you is content to stay indoors all day. Don't you crave to see what life in the fast lane is all about?'

'No. I don't.' She lowered her eyes.

'Really?' What was she hiding? Leo thought. And didn't she know that trying to keep secrets from a man was the one sure-fire way to fuel his curiosity? *His* curiosity was certainly on the move now...and he was beginning to enjoy the novelty. In fact, the weekend which had started on such an unfortunate note was definitely beginning to look up. Daniel had cracked one of those rare smiles of his, and even his mother seemed a little more relaxed than she normally did. The day so far had meandered in a more casual fashion than usual, and he had spent no time in front of his computer downloading his emails or generally continuing with business. It was proving to be all the more satisfying by the sudden challenge of ferreting out whatever Heather was keeping from him.

'You never answered my question,' he said, changing the subject so abruptly that she raised her startled blue gaze to him. 'The one about your banking knowledge. And here's another thing…' Leo leaned forward, noticing the way she flinched back warily a couple of inches in her chair. 'Last night you said that men like me take it for granted that women will want to spend time with them. What did you mean by that?'

'I didn't mean anything by it. In fact, I'm struggling to remember whether I made that remark or not.' She looked at him resentfully.

'If you deliver an insult, then you have to be prepared to back it up. What is a man like me?'

'Self-assured,' Heather told him bitterly. 'Arrogant…accustomed to giving orders and having them obeyed. Ruthless, dismissive; the sort of man who doesn't think it's wrong to use other people.'

Leo would have taken offence, but for the fact that this was more than just a casual dismissal; this was personal experience speaking. Ferociously controlled as he was, he felt a flare of sexual curiosity which took him by surprise, but he didn't fight it. He had a rich diet of very biddable women. Even women who could afford to pick and choose, women with both brains and beauty, had never been able to resist him. But he was without a woman at the moment, having parted company three months previously from the very delectable and very, very ambitious Eloise. Eloise had removed herself to New York, taking up a position with a hedge-fund company when it became obvious that their love affair wouldn't be travelling down the altar any time soon.

And there was something refreshing about this woman's candour as she glared at him with her cornflower-blue eyes, fully expecting him to hit the roof and duly confirm every scathing insult she had just listed.

'To get to the top requires a certain amount of ruthlessness.' Leo shrugged, sipped his wine and watched her over the rim of his glass.

'Maybe so, but that still doesn't make it acceptable. If you weren't so busy being ruthless, you might find that you had the time to spend with your family.'

'I will choose to overlook that,' Leo said, his expression still impassive and mildly interested, but with a hint of steel in his voice. 'Because what I really want to find out is why you're hiding here, in the middle of nowhere. What are you running from?'

'I'm not running from anything,' Heather stammered. 'And I'm not hiding. I happen to love living in the country! I don't enjoy being trapped in a building surrounded by pavements and street lights that never go off.' Behind him, Heather could see Katherine and Daniel finally making their long-overdue appearance. 'They're here,' she said, resisting the urge to groan with relief.

'Saved by the proverbial bell,' Leo murmured, but he was enjoying himself in ways he had never expected to. It occurred to him, and not for the first time, that the pursuit of money was always more rewarding than the possession of it. Eleven years ago he had made financial success his one driving ambition in life. It had eluded his parents. It had certainly eluded his brother, the mere thought of whom brought a twisted scowl of displeasure to Leo's mouth.

He had determined to prove to himself and to his parents that he could escape the cramped, stiflingly claustrophobic clutter of his lower middle-class background. Now, rich beyond his wildest dreams, he sometimes wondered whether he had managed to prove anything at all. Certainly not to his mother, even though he had been the one to bail her out of the massive debts which his father had incurred when he had chosen unwisely to invest his life savings on Alex and his ridiculous money-making ventures. He had provided her with enough financial security to last several lifetimes, and of course she was grateful—but years spent amassing his private fortune had left him with a jaded palate and a deep-rooted cynicism. Master of everything and everyone he surveyed, he had practically forgotten what it felt like to have someone ruffle his feathers.

Especially a woman—and, furthermore, a woman who could light up for seemingly everyone bar him. Right now, she was half-turned away from him, enthusing over a pair of football trainers, the must-have footwear for any aspiring footballer.

Leo leaned forward, invading her space. 'I used to play football when I was your age.'

'And you were a brilliant little footballer.' Katherine looked at her son and half-smiled. 'I remember your father taking you to your football game every Saturday morning. Do you remember that? I would stay at home with your little brother Alexander and you would trot off with your boots slung over your shoulder and a little packed lunch.'

'I remember,' Leo said gruffly. He did, now that the subject had been raised, but in truth that was a memory which had been well and truly buried.

He wasn't given to reminiscing, but he had to admit that it certainly helped to carry the conversation along. Long-forgotten football stories were brought out for the benefit of his son. Every so often as the food was brought to them Heather chipped in, although never with a personal anecdote of her own.

'You must have been to a football match or two,' Leo said lazily, pushing his empty plate away and settling his body into the chair, feet extended at an angle and lightly crossed at the ankles. 'Where did you grow up? Around here?'

'Not a million miles away,' Heather told him cautiously.

'Which would be where, exactly?'

'Reading. Near Reading, as a matter of fact.'

'Good football team there.' He looked to Daniel, including him in the conversation, making it impossible for her not to respond. 'And your family…do they still live there?'

'No. They don't. My father died years ago, and my mother remarried and moved to Portugal. She lives there now. Has a little hairdressing business.' No state secrets there, but Heather still didn't like exposing her private life to him, and she didn't know why.

'Brothers? Sisters?'

'Just me.'

'So let me get this straight…' Leo's smile made her heart beat with sickening force. 'You lived in Reading, no siblings, mother in Portugal with stepfather… What made you decide to move out here? Reading might not be one of the biggest cities in the UK, but it's still a city—still has nightclubs, restaurants, theatres, all the things that would appeal to a person of your age. In other words, you must find life pretty dead out here.'

'Stop interrogating the poor child!' Katherine said sharply, and Leo looked at his mother in amazement. When was the last time she had ever snapped at him? Normally she tiptoed around him, treating him as though he inhabited a different plane. 'You might have lots of money and power, Leonardo West, but that doesn't give you the right to do as you please with other people. You must be able to see that Heather feels uncomfortable about your probing!'

Duly chastised, Leo flushed. He noticed that his son was smirking at him.

'Which just goes to show—' he took advantage of the temporary ceasefire to draw Daniel into a conspiracy of male bonding '—that no man is safe from a nagging woman. You'll discover that for yourself in due course.'

One Disney movie and three bags of popcorn later, Heather was more than ready to make her excuses and get back to the safety of her cottage.

Her head was in a whirl. Before she had even met him, she had had some very strong, preconceived notions of Leo West: he was a selfish, egotistic workaholic who virtually ignored his mother and paid lip service to the fact that he had found himself in possession of a son, having been an absentee father for the majority of Daniel's life.

When she had finally set eyes on him, she was honest enough to admit she had been a little taken aback by the force of his personality and good looks. Having likened him to Brian in her head, she had very quickly realised that Brian was a minnow next to a man like Leo West.

After a few hours in his company, watching as some of that ferocious, icy discipline began to thaw, she was confused to find herself actually beginning to see him as more than just a comforting cardboard cutout. He was a complex, three-dimensional human being, and she didn't know whether she wanted to deal with that. Fortunately, she wouldn't have to.

Once there had been less of a necessity for her to be roped in as mediator, she had no trouble in wriggling out of the remainder of the planned evening. Daniel might not have been transformed into the loving son, but at least he seemed to have forgotten the debacle of the missed Sports Day. And Katherine…

That little show of backbone, when she had soundly ticked off Leo and spared Heather the embarrassment of being cross examined like a criminal in the dock, had been a telling reminder that she was still a mother and Leo still a son.

All told, she'd been able to leave with a pretty clear conscience.

By seven-thirty she was back in her studio. Painting had never before let her down. In the aftermath of Brian, she had retreated back to her art, and it had been a soothing balm.

Its soothing, balm-like qualities were proving more elusive now. In fact, as she peered at the fairy she had just spent forty-five minutes painting meticulously, she could swear that he bore a striking resemblance to Leo. How had that happened? And what role could a cruel, money-obsessed, self-centred workaholic fairy have in a children's book?

Having downgraded to the television—which was having a similarly non-remedial effect on her chaotic thoughts—she was startled when she heard a bang on the door.

Heather didn't think for a moment that it would be anyone but Leo, and she was shocked and frightened to discover that her heart was doing all sorts of weird things. Her head was behaving pretty badly as well, forcing her to recall the way his mouth curved in that smile that was always not very far away from cynical; the way he tilted his head to one side when he was listening to something, giving the impression that he was listening intently with every fibre of his being.

Faced with the unpalatable truth that the man had somehow managed to spark something in her that she had convinced herself was long dead and buried, Heather yanked open the door, bristling for attack.

'You've been painting again,' was the remark that greeted her. 'How are the fairies? All work and no play; you know what they say about that.'

'You keep showing up on my doorstep!'

'There's a lot to be said for predictability. Hope I'm not interrupting anything—aside from a painting jag, that is?'

'Why are you here?'

'I come bearing gifts.'

She hadn't noticed, but now he lifted both hands and she could see that he was carrying several carrier-bags.

'What's that?' Heather asked suspiciously.

'Food—Chinese. And a bottle of wine, of course. Today has worn Daniel out, and my mother has retreated to watch something on television. A historical romance; I didn't think I'd be able to stomach it.'

'And you didn't decide to work?'

'This seemed a more interesting option.' Besides, he felt in holiday mode. The day had gone well, and more than that… Leo had found himself watching her, watching the way she laughed, closing her eyes and throwing her head back, giving it everything. He watched the way she related to his mother and his son, gentle and compassionate. He had also found himself watching the way her body had shifted under her clothes, the bounce of her breasts when she had reached across to get the salt on the table…

After that illuminating little chat about the stock market, there had been no more work-related discussions, although he was pretty sure that she would rise to the challenge given half a chance. No, the conversation had been light and amusing, and he had enjoyed himself.

He had a chequered love life behind him, which was just the way he liked it. But lately he had become bored with the relentlessly intellectual conversations provided by the women he dated; bored with trying to arrange dates, with each of the women consulting their BlackBerries, endeavouring to find a suitable gap in hectic timetables, bored with leggy brunettes.

A change was as good as a rest, he had decided, and that change came in the small, curvy figure of the woman looking at him as though he might very well be something infectious.

She was a challenge, and Leo was in a mood to take on a challenge.

Furthermore, it had crossed his mind that seeing his son, and his mother for that matter, had been a considerably less stilted business with Heather in the mix. They relaxed with her in a way that they never relaxed around him. Taking on this challenge might have more than just the expected rewards.

He surfaced to the tail end of something she had been saying, and when he frowned she said very slowly, as if she were talking to someone mentally challenged, 'There was no need for you to come over here with food. You probably feel that this is a suitable thank-you gesture, but I don't need thanking.'

'Stop being so bad tempered and let me in. The food's going cold. Cold Chinese food is never a good sight—congeals.' He gave her a crooked smile. 'Besides, what's wrong with accepting a little thanks?'

It was the smile. Heather's mouth went dry and she stared at him. The sight of him took her breath away. She was aware that she was gaping, and she snapped her mouth shut and reminded herself that being deprived of breath was not a good place to be. In fact, it was terminal.

'It was a good day.' He was still smiling, his shrewd eyes taking in her response to him and banking it. She fought like a wild cat, but he got to her and, considering she got to him as well, it seemed only fitting. 'And you deserve credit for it.'

'Why are you being nice?'

'Maybe I want to show you that I'm not the self-centred, arrogant monster you seem to think I am.'

'I never said you were a monster.' She was struck by the thought that to turn him away would be to admit that her past still had a hold over her; that Brian—three years gone—still had a hold over her and could still influence the way she related to other people, other men.

'Okay.' She stood aside, making up her mind, realising that she had nothing to fear but herself and her stupid overreactions. Besides, he'd be gone in a few hours. 'But I really have to get back to my painting some time tonight.'

Leo stepped inside, brushing her protestations aside, and headed for the kitchen. Unerringly he knew where it would be, and felt her walking behind him; he liked the anticipation of what the evening might bring. Sure there was a lot to be said for predictability, but there was a great deal more to be said for the thrill of the unknown, and her obvious reluctance to be anywhere near him had roused his hunting instincts.

He dumped the bags on the table. The wine was still cold from the fridge.

'If you point to the plates…'

'Don't tell me that you're Mr Domestic?'

'You mean you wouldn't believe me?' He perched against the counter, arms folded, and laughed softly under his breath.

'I mean—' Heather had to take a deep breath to steady her sudden giddiness '—I'd quicker believe that there were lots of little green people dashing about on planet Mars.'

'Okay. You win.' He gave a mock gesture of defeat. 'Domesticity doesn't agree with me.' He watched as she opened the bottle of wine and poured them both a glass. The ubiquitous flowing skirt was gone. She was wearing some grey jogging-bottoms and an off-white vest bearing the tell-tale signs of her painting. For the first time, he could really see something of her figure, and his eyes roved appreciatively over the full breasts, the flat stomach, the womanly curve of her hips. She was by no means thin, but her body was toned and surprisingly tanned. He wondered whether she had been taking advantage of the hot weather, tanning in her garden— tanning nude in her garden…?

When she swung round to give him a glass, he surprised himself by flushing.

'And why is that?' Heather asked. 'Could it be that, the more money a person has, the more temptation there is to buy the services of other people who are a lot more handy at doing all those inconvenient chores like cooking?'

Instead of bringing down his shutters, that little undercurrent of belligerence sent a jolt of red-hot lust running through him.

'Ah…' He strolled towards her and took a sip of wine. 'But just think, my little economist, of how many people I keep employed…'

Looking up at him, she could feel that breathing thing happening again. She forced herself to get a grip, to bring the conversation back down to a level she could handle.

'Or maybe you're just scared at the thought of putting down roots,' she said wryly. 'And if you never treat your house like a home then you never put down roots, do you?'

CHAPTER THREE

HUGE inroads had been made into the Chinese food, which was spread on the table between them. Noodles and other assorted bits of food had managed to escape the chopsticks and were hardening on the pine table-top. The bottle of wine was nearing its end, but Heather was barely aware of having drunk anything at all. It had taken a little while, but she had lowered her defences and was proud of how normal she was behaving. As far as exercises went, this was a pretty good result. Yes, she could talk to the man without pigeon-holing him. She knew him for what he was, but was not letting that get in the way of responding to him like an adult. She was smugly aware of a sense of personal achievement.

Of course, it had to be said that Leo was making things easy for her. He was no longer on the attack, no longer looking at her with narrow-eyed suspicion which made her hackles rise. The conversation was light, skimming the surface, avoiding any pitfalls.

And the wine was helping. Heather rested her elbow on the table, cupped her face in her hand and looked at Leo sleepily.

'Don't tell me that you're going to doze off in the middle of my conversation?' he said, sipping his wine and looking at her over the rim of his glass. 'My ego would never recover.'

'And we both know that you've got a very healthy one of those,' Heather murmured. His eyes were hypnotic. She could stare into them for ever.

'I'm going to say thank you, even though I have a sneaking suspicion that there wasn't anything complimentary behind the observation.'

'My head feels a little woolly.'

'In which case, we'd better get you to the sitting room. Leave all this debris. I'll tidy it up.'

'You will? You're domestically challenged—you said that yourself. Do you even know what a dishwasher looks like?'

Leo gave a low laugh and looked at her. She was as soft and full as a peach. Her hair was a riot of gold ringlets framing her face, giving her a look that was impossibly feminine. No hard edges there. Sitting across from her as they had eaten had required a lot of restraint. He had watched her as she tipped her head back, her eyes half-closed, so that she could savour the noodles on her chopsticks, and he had had to shift his body because it had been so damned uncomfortable dealing with his aching erection.

'You seem to forget that I had a childhood,' he told her drily. 'And there was no one around then to do my bidding. My brother and I had our list of chores every day, and some of them included clearing the table after meals.' Another memory that had not surfaced for a very long time.

'I can't imagine you doing chores. I bet you paid your brother to do yours for you.' Heather had never met Alex. She knew that he was away somewhere distant and exotic and had been for a while.

'Come on. I'm going to get you into the sitting room.' The shutters had come down with the mention of his brother, and he stood up. But as she pushed herself away from the table he moved quickly around, and was sweeping her off her feet, taking her by surprise and therefore finding little resistance.

After a few startled seconds, Heather wriggled against him. 'What are you *doing*?'

'I'm carrying you into your sitting room. You look a little wobbly on your feet.'

'I'm perfectly capable of walking three inches!'

'Stop struggling.'

'You'll pull a muscle in your back, lifting me up!' After all her smug satisfaction at how amazingly adult she had been—chatting to Leo as though he was just another perfectly normal guy who didn't rattle her cage—she could now feel every nerve ending in her body screaming in response to this physical contact. His chest was hard and muscular and the hands supporting her were strong and sinewy; all those stirrings, of whatever the heck they were that she didn't want, were flooding through her in a tidal wave.

The more she wriggled, the more the stirring magnified, so she stopped wriggling and told herself to get a grip.

'There.' Leo deposited her gently on the squashy sofa in the sitting room and stood back, looking down at her. 'Ordeal over.' He wasn't sure whether to be amused or disgruntled at her frantic efforts to bolt.

'It wasn't an *ordeal*,' Heather told him, gathering herself into a sitting position. 'I was— I was just *concerned* for you…' Her heartbeat should have been returning to normal, but it wasn't.

'Concerned?'

'I'm not the lightest person in the world.' She spelled it out for him, willing herself to get back into sensible, protective mode.

Leo sat on the sofa and she immediately squirmed into a cross-legged position, her hands resting lightly on her knees.

'I have no idea what you're talking about.'

'It doesn't matter.'

'You do that.'

'What?'

'Introduce a topic and then suddenly decide to back off before you can explain what you're talking about.'

'There's nothing to explain.' She gave a careless shrug and linked her fingers together. 'I just think that caveman gestures like that are probably better done with someone skinnier than me. Probably with one of those women who fall over themselves to be in your company.'

Leo, well skilled in the ways of women, could recognise a fishing expedition from a mile away. She was curious about him, wanted to know more, but was reluctant to frame her questions directly. Good sign.

'I thought women liked the caveman approach.'

'Not when it can lead to personal injury.'

'Who on earth ever told you that you were…?'

'Fat?' Heather supplied for him. 'Overweight?' She stared at her fingers. 'In need of losing a few pounds? No one.'

'No one. Well, you can tell *no one* that he was way off-target. You are neither fat nor are you overweight. And as for all those women who fall over themselves to be in my company…' He noticed the way she inclined her head very slightly, as if stilling to hear some distant sound. This, he thought with satisfaction, was the sound of a woman who was sexually interested in a man. 'They do tend to be on the skinny side,' he admitted. He relaxed back on the sofa and crossed his legs.

'I knew it.'

'One more of those monstrously predictable things about me?'

'Why is it that men with lots of money are always attracted

to women who look as though they would have difficulty keeping upright in a strong wind? I mean, really, is there something *attractive* about a human being who doesn't eat?'

Leo laughed, and when he was finished laughing he looked at her and shook his head, as if a little dazed by the woman sitting opposite him on the sofa.

'No, there's absolutely nothing attractive about a woman who doesn't eat, and I have to admit that I've dated a lot of those.'

'Brainless bimbos?' She wanted to pull information out of him, and was guiltily aware that she was being as intrusive with him as he had been with her.

'Brainless bimbos? No, definitely not that.'

Now, that *did* surprise her, and Leo laughed again, amused. 'Why would I be attracted to a brainless bimbo?' he asked.

'Because she looks good on your arm?'

'And what about when there's no one around to see her looking good on my arm? What conversation could there possibly be with a brainless bimbo?'

'So what sort of women *do* you go out with?'

'Why do you ask?'

Why, Heather thought, do *I ask?* This wasn't the sort of casual, skimming-the-surface conversation which was safe and unthreatening. There was an edge to this conversation, but like someone standing on the edge of a precipice, peering down, she found that it was irresistible.

'No reason. Just making conversation. Really, though, you should go. I'm awfully tired. There's honestly no need for you to tidy the kitchen. I can do that later, or better still in the morning.'

Leo had no intention of leaving, but it dawned on him that Heather was not like any other woman he had known. That bristly, belligerent spark wasn't an act to get his attention. If she told him that he should go, then she meant it, and since Leo wasn't going anywhere—at least not yet—he stood up and shook his head in his best bedside manner, something of which he'd had precious little practice.

'You need some coffee.' Before she could launch into another goodbye speech, he left the room, only throwing over his shoulder that maybe she should doze for a bit. The occasional catnap could work wonders, he told her. Not that he knew, but it was all part of the bedside manner.

In truth, Leo had forgotten the art of seduction, or at least the art of persuasion.

With women, the outcome was usually apparent within a matter of minutes: conversation of the intelligent variety, a certain type of eye contact and then the unspoken assumption that they would end up as lovers.

With Heather, he realised that one false move and she would run a mile—and of course, given that he was no more than a highly competitive red-blooded male, what more of a turn on could there be than an uncertain outcome?

Not for a minute did it occur to Leo that a deliberate seduction was anything less than perfectly reasonable. He took his time in the kitchen. Dishes were washed and precariously balanced on the draining board, because drying and putting them away seemed a senseless waste of time when they would be used again at some point in the future—and she had been right with the 'dishwasher' accusation. There was some sort of coffee-making machine with nozzles and a vaguely threatening glass jug, which he ignored. Instead, he made them both a cup of instant coffee and was gratified to find that she wasn't dozing, as he'd suspected she might be, when he returned to the sitting room.

'Instant,' he said, handing her the cup and then sitting on

one of the big, comfortable chairs by the fireplace. 'There was a machine there, but…'

'But you didn't have a clue how to use it?' She cupped the mug between her hands and watched him as he sat back, relaxed, in the chair.

'I could have figured it out in time.' He shot her a wicked grin that made her toes curl. 'But life's too short to waste any of it trying to come to grips with a complicated machine that just ends up making stuff you can get out of a jar.'

'It tastes much better than the stuff you can get out of a jar.' After their very civilised evening, Heather knew that she should really be getting rid of him. He had made a nice gesture; she had not been churlish and thrown it back at him, and now she could close the evening on a satisfactory note. But didn't it make her feel alive, having him here? Looking at him? It was, in equal measure, exciting and disturbing.

'That's open to debate.' But he laughed again. 'Tell me about your work. Do you work freelance, or are you commissioned to a publisher?'

Since this was nice, safe conversation, Heather felt herself relax as she began explaining to him what she did, telling him about some of the books she had illustrated, then finding that they were talking about art in general. Working freelance as she did, she had relatively little contact with members of the opposite sex, and for the past three years that had suited her. After Brian, she had retreated to lick her wounds, only meeting the occasional guy through some of the women she had befriended in the town, mums from the school where she gave art lessons to their kids once a week. She had accepted no dates, and indeed had made sure to give off all the right 'hands off' signals to anyone who had looked even mildly interested.

It made a change to have male company. That, she told

herself, was why she was now talking to Leo. She had allowed him in to prove to herself that she was capable of rising above her past. Also, it made sense for them to be, if not friends, then at least on speaking terms, because she would bump into him now and again, and the less awkwardness between them the better.

She resolutely slammed the door on the little voice telling her that she was enjoying that weird, tingly, excited flutter inside her; that she was turned on by his charisma, mesmerised by the raw power of his sex appeal.

Heather was not in the market for being turned on or mesmerised by anyone. In due course, she would emerge from the protective walls she had built around herself and would get back into the dating scene. If she wasn't too old by then. And, when she did, she would be very careful about the type of men she went out with. In fact, she might get them to fill out a questionnaire before the first date—nothing too complicated, just a few sheets of questions so that she could make sure that only the right kind of guy got through the net.

Since Leo was the complete opposite of the right kind of guy, she felt herself fully protected. Yes, she could appreciate all that alpha-male sex appeal; yes, she could admit that he was ferociously intelligent. But there was no way that she could ever physically be attracted to him, not when her head told her that it made no sense—and she was always careful to be guided by her head now.

So why shouldn't she enjoy talking to someone who seemed interested in her art? In fact, she even found herself showing him some of her past illustrations, ones she had done for a trilogy about a ballerina.

'So you don't just do the fairies,' Leo murmured, impressed

by what he saw, but not liking the way the evening was descending ever increasingly into friendly chit-chat. 'Tell me something, do you make a living from this?'

'Depends on what you call "a living".' Heather stashed her portfolio to the side of the sofa and sat back down. 'Compared to what you probably earn, I don't even begin to make a living, but then again I realised a long time ago that money's way overrated.'

'Yes?' Leo's ears pricked up. 'Tell me about it.' He stood up and began pacing the small room, pausing to look at pictures in frames, eventually settling on the sofa with her. Sitting on the opposite side of the room was not working for him. In a minute she would be gearing up to remind him of how tired she was before she sent him on his way.

His frustration levels were growing by the second.

'There's nothing to tell,' Heather said casually. 'You just have to read about all those super-rich, super-privileged people who end up in rehab all the time. I mean, have you ever thought that *you* might end up in rehab one day?'

Distracted from his intention to go beyond the harmless conversation about art and culture and steer them into edgier waters, Leo raised his eyebrows, amused.

'I'll admit, that that's one thing I've never worried about.'

'Why not?' Heather looked at him thoughtfully. She could feel every nerve in her body on red alert. It wasn't a massive sofa, and, now that he had plonked himself on it, it seemed to have shrunk to the size of a pin cushion. If she stretched her foot out just a tiny bit it would make contact with his thigh, so she was making very sure to huddle into herself. Her knees were drawn up to her chest and her arms were firmly clasped around them.

'Why should I? In case you hadn't noticed, I'm not a loser. People end up in rehab when they've lost control of their lives.'

'Or when they're lonely, maybe. Then they take refuge in all sorts of things.'

'But I'm not lonely, and the concept of taking refuge in anything is abhorrent to me. I have no time for people who waste their lives in drugs or alcohol. And how did we get onto this anyway?'

'Because I said that money can buy a lot of things, but it doesn't buy happiness.' She looked at him and her breath caught in her throat. The sun had dipped, and the long shadows in the room accentuated the angles of his face, the beautiful, harsh set of his features. Their easy banter had lulled her into a false sense of security, she realised. She had silenced those nagging little voices at the back of her mind, but they had re-surfaced with double their vigour, telling her that she could pretend to feel in control, but underneath the pretence was the reality that she was attracted to him. Staring at him like a dumbstruck teenager was just one of the things she wanted to do. The rest brought her out in a cold sweat.

'I mean,' she said, poised to redress the balance, 'you're rich, and yet can you honestly say that you're completely happy?'

Leo raked restless fingers through his dark hair and wondered how he had managed to get caught on the back foot. 'Yes, I can, but I expect you're going to tell me that actually I'm not.'

'You can't be completely satisfied with your relationship with Katherine and Daniel,' Heather said flatly. She regretted her outburst the minute it left her lips, but it was too late, and she conceded that it might be the only way to fight the dawning realisation that she was attracted to the worst possible man for her.

'I'm working on that,' Leo grated. 'And enough said on that subject.'

'I think it's time you went, Leo.' Heather stood up and

made a pretence of yawning. 'I'm shattered. I'm not accustomed to drinking, and it's made me feel really sleepy. Thank you for coming over and for bringing a meal for me, and I'm glad that we've managed to…get over our initial differences.' She took up a defensive position by the door, standing to one side and watching in silence as Leo finally took the hint and stood up, although it had to be said that he didn't look in a frantic rush to leave. His eyes tangled with hers and she looked away nervously.

'I think we've done more than just *get over our initial differences*,' he murmured, walking towards her.

'Um…' Heather felt the words dry up in her throat with each step closer to her that he took.

'I think that we got over our initial differences some time earlier today, in fact. It might have been in the cinema, when you absent-mindedly helped yourself to some of my popcorn.'

Heather flushed. His voice was low, sexy and coaxing, and there was a lazy, speculative look in his eyes that made her feel hot and self-conscious—although she wasn't sure why, because all he was talking about, for goodness' sake, was a bag of popcorn!

'I didn't think you'd noticed,' she mumbled, glancing away, because his eyes seemed to be boring holes in her. Hadn't anyone ever told him that it was rude to stare? 'I have a problem with popcorn. I always feel that I can do without it, but the minute the movie starts I realise I can't.'

She could feel his eyes still on her, making her even more horribly aware of her inadequate dress-code. Her shameless probing had not managed to elicit a huge amount about his love life, but she had managed to glean that he appreciated women who were slim and brainy. Slim, brainy women would not be caught dead in a pair of old jogging-bottoms and a tee shirt, even if they were comfortable. Slim, brainy women relaxed in designer jeans and super-expensive blouses with pearl buttons, maybe a silk scarf casually draped around their necks. She had met a fair few slim, brainy women in her time and they had all spoken with cut-glass accents and looked like beautiful, porcelain mannequins.

She realised that she wanted to find out more about these women. Was there one on the scene now, waiting back in London for Leo to return from doing his paternal duties?

She slammed the door shut on her curiosity and adopted a bright smile.

'What time do you leave tomorrow?' she asked. 'Have you got any plans for Daniel? I know he really enjoyed today; I could tell. He's not the most talkative child on the face of the earth, but you can always see when he's in a good mood and he was in a very good mood, today. I'm very proud of you. You made a big effort after having missed his Sports Day and he appreciated it. Kids are like that. They don't harbour grudges or have long memories…' He was looking less and less impressed the longer her eulogy continued, until she finally faltered into an uncertain silence.

'You're very *proud* of me?'

'Well, yes…'

'I'm not ten years old, Heather. Obviously it's heart warming to know that you're *proud* of me, but…' This time he did more than just allow his eyes to linger on her face, to travel the length of her small, voluptuous body. He reached out and placed his hand behind her neck. There was nothing passionate about the gesture. He remained where he was, leaning against the wall, feet lightly crossed at the ankles. With anyone else, it would have felt almost fraternal. With Leo, it felt as though he had stripped her of her clothes and ordered her to do an erotic dance. The wobbly legs which she had earlier put down to a glass too much of wine now felt like jelly, and every shameful, idiotic, indecent tug of attraction which she had managed to airbrush away surfaced with red-hot ferocity through her veins. She felt weak and dizzy from the force of it all, and she half-closed her eyes as she drew in her breath unevenly.

Leo could feel reluctance mixed with desire in those few seconds as he detailed her reaction to his touch with an expert eye.

She had thoroughly disapproved of him at their first meeting and hadn't been able to resist the opportunity to lecture. Now, he had succeeded in becoming the star pupil. Add to that the fact that she was probably very innocent in her experiences with men, cooped up as she was in the middle of nowhere, and he really wasn't that surprised that she was now licking her lips nervously. If he wasn't mistaken, she was trembling a little, like the fragile petal of a flower being blown by a very slight breeze.

He brushed the pad of his thumb against the soft, sensitive skin of her neck and then tangled his fingers in her hair, which was as soft as silk.

'But…' He was finding it hard to remember what he was saying. He was finding it hard, in fact, to think coherently, which was a novelty for him and gave him a certain buzz. 'There are far more satisfying ways you could use to reward my Brownie points.' The hand which had been plunged into her glorious golden curls now moved to trace the contours of her neckline, which was pretty frustrating for him, because, whilst her close-fitting tee shirt proudly advertised the bounty it shielded, the round neckline made damn sure that his wandering fingers couldn't get anywhere near it.

Heather stared at him, her lips parted. Her brain was having trouble keeping pace with the bizarre turn of events. In a series of rapid, thumbnail clips, she mentally went over the evening, starting with his unexpected arrival, Chinese food in hand, and travelling down the enjoyable few hours they had spent—him being ultra-nice and ultra-interested in everything she had to say while she watched him surreptitiously from under her lashes and told herself that everything was normal, that it made perfect sense to be friendly, because that was how good neighbours should be.

She knew he was going to kiss her. For a few seconds, all rational thought went into free fall as he dipped her head back, and then his mouth was on hers, urgent, hungry, demanding, pressing her back against the wall.

As the walls of her resistance such as there had been came tumbling down, Leo felt a surge of lust and triumph. Against his, her body was as soft as he had imagined. Her breasts were squashed against his chest, and with a groan he pushed his hands under the tee shirt, sliding them effortlessly out of her stretchy bra and then losing himself in their abundance.

It was enough to galvanise Heather into horrified action. In the space of a few reckless minutes, she had succumbed to a need that was so powerful it overwhelmed all her ability to think rationally.

The touch of his hands on her breasts was like an urgent wake-up call and she pushed him back, scrambling in her desperation to regain her composure.

She was no match for him in the strength stakes, but she had the element of surprise on her side. The very last thing Leo had expected was to find himself repelled at the very height of his excitement.

'Go. Now.' She had awkwardly pulled the tee shirt back

into some semblance of order, and her arms were folded protectively across her breasts. On any other occasion, his look of disbelief would have had her laughing.

'*Go? Now?* If this is your version of playing hard to get, then it won't work.'

'I'm not playing hard to get. I'm asking you to leave. I shouldn't have…'

'Led me on?'

'I did *not* lead you on!'

'Don't play the outraged virgin with me. I've seen the way you've stolen looks at me, the way you've reacted when I've been within touching distance of you!'

Heather, guilty and appalled, stared at him mutely. 'I'm sorry,' she mumbled, unable to deny the charge, but likewise refusing to admit to it. 'If you thought that I was leading you on, then you've got hold of the wrong end of the stick. That's the last thing I intended to do.'

'What was your intention, in that case?'

'I…'

'Because I don't hear you denying that what I felt here was a case of mutual attraction.' Leo was half-stunned to hear himself demanding an explanation from her, demanding to know why she hadn't immediately and without question fallen into bed with him. He hadn't been mistaken about the way she felt about him, the attraction that sizzled below the surface of their amicable exchanges. He was never wrong about things like that. When it came to second guessing female vibes, he could have written a book on the subject.

What he was inexperienced at was having to deal with a woman who felt the attraction and then came up short on the follow-through.

'Not all of us treat sex as a casual indulgence,' Heather told him shakily, backing away to escape the stranglehold of his powerful personality.

'You have no idea how I treat sex.'

'I can risk a guess—no strings, no commitments, something that hits the spot and then, when it stops hitting the spot, becomes disposable—like a Chinese takeaway, in other words. You're not domestic because you don't have to be, and I'll damn sure bet you're never even remotely domestic in the presence of a woman just in case she gets nesting ideas. Am I right?'

'And maybe there's a damn good reason for that,' Leo heard himself say grittily. 'Maybe I've learnt a couple of things about the joys of commitment. Maybe I've learnt that it's just not what it's cracked up to be, and I'm the kind of guy who learns lessons very fast. Some might say at the speed of light.'

He stared down at her and was as surprised at this admission as she appeared to be, judging from the wide-eyed look on her face. It was one of the rare moments when mention of his wife had been uttered on his lips, the last time being when she had died in the car crash in Australia, thereby catapulting his life into another lane. Even then, when the past had resurged into his present, he had conducted affairs with a businesslike approach, spurning all invitations from his mother to open up. On that swift and relentless rise to the top, Leo had discarded all possible weaknesses, and that included any maudlin tendencies to confide. Not that he had ever really had any. The sensitive role had been his brother's domain.

Maybe it was the silence that greeted his unexpected admission that encouraged him to continue. Or maybe it was the fact that she was reaching to play the moral trump-card again and he refused to allow himself to be boxed in.

He couldn't quite put his finger on it, but he said with

cutting cynicism, 'My ex-wife taught me some very valuable lessons, one of which was that life can get messy, complicated and downright ugly the minute a person makes the mistake of thinking that sex is better, more worthwhile, when a little love or infatuation is thrown into the mix.'

'What are you trying to say?'

'I'm trying to say that there's no virtue in self-denial because the happy-ever-after scenario isn't waiting just around the corner.'

Heather couldn't disagree with that. She couldn't, however, see the only alternative as throwing herself into whatever passing attraction she might happen to feel for any man.

'Well?' Leo prompted harshly, angry with himself for sinking so low as to explain his motivations, and angry with her because he had expected her to launch into a diatribe about love, romance and all that other rubbish which seemed to propel couples up the aisle only to find themselves racing for the divorce courts three years later.

'Well, what?' They stared at each other. Heather could hardly breathe, and she was holding her body so still that she could very well have grown roots. Eventually, she said quietly, 'Would you like another cup of coffee?'

For a split second, Leo hesitated. He had done more than was acceptable to him. Unbelievably, he had been rejected in his advances, and worse than that had not turned and walked away. It was what he should have done and what he would have expected himself to do. It wasn't as though there weren't other women around. In fact, he had files of them. But this one… Something about her turned him on so massively that he gave a curt nod and followed her into the kitchen, watching as she fiddled with the ridiculous coffee-making gadget so that she could produce two cups of superior coffee in a matter of seconds. It tasted nothing like the dishwater he had produced for her.

The fact that she had offered him the cup of coffee, which even now he was accepting with a slight inclination of his head, led him to believe that his words had struck a chord with her.

As they ought to! he considered.

'What did your wife do to leave you so bitter?'

'Details are unimportant.'

'Do you really think so?' Heather said sadly. 'Sometimes I think they're the most important things.'

'In that case, I'll tell you. My dearest wife enjoyed the fruits of my labours, but not the work entailed in providing them. She needed more than just a limitless bank account. She needed constant, round-the-clock flattery, and when I wasn't around to provide it she found others who could. She was beautiful. She was rich. She had a great deal of choice. Hence my scepticism about the wonders of love and marriage.'

'I'm sorry. It must have been awful for you. But when Daniel was born didn't you both try to…stitch things together? Give it a go?'

But Leo was done with answering questions and dwelling on his miserable, short-lived marriage. Instead he turned his mind to the glorious, contrary woman sitting opposite him, her brow knitted in a compassionate frown.

This sordid story, one which he had never told a soul, would have fractured her rosy picture of human relationships. It also would have made her see that what he had offered her—a satisfying relationship based on the one thing that made any sense—was not to be discarded. In fact, he was pretty sure that she had come to that conclusion herself even before his unprecedented confession.

The option of having her step down from her high horse and come to him, only to taste the same rejection that she had dished out to him, wasn't even considered.

He wanted her and he wasn't going to play any games. But the sound of her acquiescence would be truly sweet indeed.

CHAPTER FOUR

LEO relaxed. When it came to relationships, things had a disturbing tendency to become mundane once that brief pursuit was over, but he had a feeling that Heather would be different. Maybe it was because she was unwittingly involved in a side of his life to which none of his other women had been introduced. He had always made sure to keep London and the country very far apart. He bedded and entertained his women in the city. The country was for the family side of him, which had been hugely sidelined over the years, but which would always be there, more so now that Daniel had arrived on the scene. It was the first time he had ever considered the possibility of dating someone who knew his family. Frankly, he had never been in the country long enough to meet anyone, but even if he had he would have run a mile. He had never seen that, all things considered, there were certain advantages to the situation, especially now that Daniel was around.

High on the plus side would be the fact that dates wouldn't have to be made with the precision timing of a military campaign. Investment bankers and barristers were all well and good, but trying to arrange dates was usually a hellish business. He was busy, so were they and there had been more than one occasion when, having met and invariably spent the evening discussing aspects of work, he'd just been so damned tired that he could hardly be bothered to enjoy what should have been the highlight of the evening.

With Heather, it would be different. She was anchored in the country. He had a rosy image of her waiting there for him, waiting for her man. The idea of a roast in the oven was taking things a little too far, but it would really make a pleasant change to down-pedal a bit. He didn't know how much experience she had of city life but he would bet that the closest she had ever come to it would have been on television. The simplicity of what she had to offer would be a breath of fresh air. Heck, he might even bring her up to London now and again, take her to a play or some such thing, open her eyes to the big, bad world out there.

The more Leo thought about it, the more he figured that he needed a restful relationship, at least for the time being. What could be more restful than an artist, someone in tune with Nature? And yet wrapped up in such a sexy package that just thinking of her sent his mind further south.

Add to that the fact that time spent with his mother and Daniel was infinitely easier when she was in the mix, and Leo was satisfied that he had done the right thing in accepting the cup of coffee that was even now going slightly tepid. He took a sip and made some inconsequential remark about her being right, that the complicated coffee-making machine really did live up to its spec.

At the same time, his eyes lingered over her flushed face tinged with pink, the full breasts… God, when he thought about touching them again—not just a schoolboy grope under a tee shirt, but stripping her of her clothes and lavishing them with his full, undivided attention—spending time, taking those rosebud nipples into his mouth and hearing her moan as he suckled on them…

'I'm surprised we didn't meet sooner.' He tore himself away from his erotic, meandering thoughts.

'Are you? Why?'

'You live just round the corner, so to speak. I would have expected Katherine to have invited you up to the house for a meal.'

'You mean on a weekend? When you happened to be down?'

Leo didn't much care for the way she said that—*when you happened to be down*—but he let it go. He was in an extremely good mood now and he wasn't going to jeopardise it over a dodgy tone of voice.

'You weren't down very often, though, were you? I mean, how often did you visit your mother before Daniel arrived?'

'I have a lot of work commitments, as I think I've mentioned to you before,' Leo said, standing up to pour himself another mug of coffee and then returning to the chair, angling it to one side so that he could stretch out his legs. He could think of better things to do than talking, now that their differences were settled, but since talking seemed to be on the agenda he might just as well make himself as comfortable as he could. 'It's always very difficult finding time. I'm abroad a lot. I've never been a nine to five kind of guy. Sure, some are content with that, but there's no gain without pain.' He shrugged. 'That's just the way it is.'

Heather knew that all too well. That kiss, that mistake that she had allowed to happen, had caught her off-balance, but she was back in control now. She had to be. She also had to explain to him why she had pushed him away, and not so much because she was a fair-minded creature who felt some deep need to justify her actions. Heck, she doubted Leo West had ever justified his actions to anybody on the face of the earth! If there was one man to whom she need never justify herself, it was him. No, she had to explain because she had to hear herself verbalise all the reasons why she would never, ever have anything to do with a man like him. She had started seeing little sides to him, and every small glimpse had lowered her defences, and that just wasn't going to do.

It surprised her that he had taken rejection so well. In fact, she was astounded that he had actually agreed to come into the kitchen, have a cup of coffee and hear her out. She could only think that he must have the attitude of 'win a few, lose a few'. Or maybe he was so unaccustomed to any form of rejection from a woman that he felt compelled to hear her explain her behaviour.

Heather had no real idea why he had made a pass at her in the first place. She wasn't his type. She could only conclude that it was because he was a highly sexed male and he had tuned in to her unconscious fascination with him and interpreted that as availability. Available women were the curse of the wealthy man. He probably hadn't even stopped to think that he might not be able to just reach out and take whatever he saw and happened to want at that particular point in time, like a kid in a sweet shop with too much pocket money to spend.

'Why did you decide to send Daniel to school here?' she asked, changing the subject, wanting him to confirm with every sentence why she had been crazy to allow him to creep between the chink in her armour. 'I mean, why didn't you keep him with you, in London? There must have been hundreds of schools you could have sent him to.'

Leo frowned. 'Where are we going with all this?'

'We're having a conversation. Is there something wrong with that? I'm just expressing curiosity about the choices you made.'

'I couldn't have Daniel in London with me,' Leo told her

abruptly. 'You have to understand that my life there is not tailored for the inclusion of a child.'

Heather was nodding. She could believe that one, all right.

'Even if there had been a permanent *au pair* on tap, there would still have remained the question of my working hours. I'm out of the country fifty percent of the time. Empires don't run themselves; they need a captain at the helm. I'm that captain, and I'm steering a vast ship. I have offices in New York, Madrid and China, to name but a few. There would have been no consistency and that wouldn't have been fair to Daniel. I felt it far better that he settle in the country where he could have the benefit of my mother being permanently there for him.'

'That sounds incredibly convenient for you.'

'It made sense at the time.' Leo fought down his impatience, which he knew would get him nowhere fast.

'Did it make sense to Daniel?'

Leo's eyes narrowed. 'Maybe we could leave the question-and-answer session for another day?'

'Is that because you just don't fancy answering my questions because they make you feel uncomfortable?'

'You've already shared your thoughts with me on my relationship with Daniel. Frankly, I don't see the point of going over old ground.' He sought to hang on to his good humour, to think of what lay ahead. 'Today was a good day. The best day I've had with him since he came to England, in fact. Why analyse and dissect the past when it's so much more worthwhile to build on the present?'

'Okay.'

Leo relaxed. This was more like it. Bit of a shame that they were separated by the width of the kitchen table. If they hadn't been, he would have translated his relaxation into something a little more tangible, would have drawn her into him, seduced her with his mouth and his hands and smothered all her nagging concerns with his lips. Of course, she would have her nagging concerns. She had made those perfectly obvious the first time they had met, and they wouldn't have evaporated just because it had been a successful day out. He strove to understand and make allowances for someone whose personality was so wildly different from his own.

She was an innocent, someone whose lack of life experiences had given her a childishly disingenuous outlook on life. It was both charming and disconcerting at the same time. Add to that the sort of bluntness that would send most men running a mile, and the combination was incendiary. Since he wasn't most men, though, he felt well equipped to deal with her. In fact, it was all part and parcel of the package that was so irresistibly attractive. Those first signs of irritability vanished before the pleasing prospect of harnessing all that fire and making it his; a change from cool, intellectual, sophisticated power women was long overdue.

'Good,' he said with satisfaction. 'So…where do we go from here? I suggest somewhere a bit more comfortable than the kitchen.'

Heather looked at him, at the lazy smile curving his lips, at the unspoken suggestion behind his fabulous eyes, and the vague questions she had asked herself were suddenly answered in an instant of comprehension.

Leo hadn't politely taken rejection because he was indifferent, and he hadn't accepted a cup of coffee because he was eaten up with curiosity to hear why she had pushed him away.

How could she have been foolish enough to think that? He just wasn't built that way. He had accepted a cup of coffee because he had assumed it heralded her acquiescence, and he wouldn't have been in the least surprised at that because he was so used to getting what he wanted.

'Where do you have in mind?' she asked with a shuttered expression.

'Well…we could start in the sitting room and progress to the bedroom. Although, if you're really stuck on staying here…' He shot her a wolfish smile that made her stomach do a back flip and reminded her powerfully of why, exactly, he was so dangerous for her.

'If we stay in here?' she prompted. 'What? A quick romp against the kitchen units?'

The smile dropped from Leo's face. 'Poor use of words.'

'It doesn't matter how you wrap it up, that's what you're suggesting, isn't it? Or we could go upstairs to the bedroom. Might last a bit longer there.' She thought of them together on her king-sized bed with its floral duvet; she thought of the floral duvet being kicked off in the heat of the moment and shakily closed the door on the image. It was way too easy for her imagination to break its reins and run rampant.

'Why don't you let me show you? You can tell me afterwards whether you have any complaints. I guarantee you won't.'

'Because you're so sure of yourself?'

'Correct.'

'Conceited, aren't you?'

'Not conceited. I just don't see the point of hiding behind false modesty.'

Two patches of bright colour had appeared on her cheeks, and the hand wrapped round the mug was trembling. She set the mug down and clasped her hands together on her lap out of sight. The atmosphere between them sizzled like a live wire. She had expected him to be enraged by her slurs on his skills as a lover, and was now disproportionately shaken by the fact that he hadn't been.

'And then, after we've made love, what happens next? You return to London, feeling refreshed? Just out of interest, do you return to London to share your fabulous love-making skills with another woman? Maybe more than one?'

'Do you want a fight, Heather? Is that it?'

'I'm just curious.'

'Well, to satisfy your curiosity, I don't happen to be involved with anyone else at the moment, and in case you're not getting the message loud and clear I don't spread myself thin when it comes to women. The idea of having a harem of women on the go is repugnant.'

'So what *does* happen, in that case—after today?'

'Is that what's worrying you? You think that you might be a one-night stand? Well, let me put your mind to rest on that score—I don't do one-night stands. I don't do flocks of women because they happen to be available. I have a libido but I also have self-control.'

'But you don't do permanence, either.'

'No. I don't.'

'And how have all those women you've dated felt about that? Have they all conveniently shared your aversion to taking the plunge?' Like a dog with a bone, she was finding it difficult to let it go. She wanted him gone, but she didn't. She wanted to tell him her point of view, but she couldn't curb her desire to hear his. She hated her curiosity, but it was like an itch that needed to be scratched. She was desperate to get her anger to boiling point, because she would really have liked to despise him, but little pieces of him that didn't fit in with the stereotype kept sabotaging all her efforts, and her body was betraying her mind and ambushing her good intentions.

'I make it clear from the outset that a wedding ring isn't part of the agenda. If some of them have nursed any hopes in that direction, then they haven't said. I don't go out with women who throw hissy fits if they think they've been let down, and I don't go out with women who think that marriage is the inevitable conclusion to a relationship. Does that answer your question?'

'So all's fair in love and war?'

'Get to the point, Heather.' The tepid coffee was now stone cold. Leo pushed it aside and looked at her. Having dived into the water, he was only now realising that there were icebergs under the surface. He'd never had to put this amount of effort into a woman before, he thought ill-temperedly.

'The point is…' There was a jumble of words in her head and she was temporarily silenced as she tried to sift through them, find the words that were important and discard the ones that weren't.

She could feel his cool, watchful eyes on her and she wished that she could read what he was thinking. Why did he have to be so damned complex? Why couldn't he have done her the favour of just fitting into the handy box in her head?

'The point is…' She stood up awkwardly. 'Look, I can't have this type of conversation here.'

'Oh, but I thought the kitchen was the best bet.'

'If you don't want to hear what I have to say, then that's fine. You know where the door is.'

'Oh, don't think you're going to get off that easily,' Leo grated. 'I can't wait to hear what you have to say.'

He followed her into the sitting room where she proceeded to stand by the window, hugging herself and keeping as far away from him as possible. Outbursts and melodrama were two things he had no time for, but for some reason wild horses wouldn't have dragged him away from whatever lame story was about to unfold. If this was some kind of ruse to inveigle him into making promises he would inevitably fail to keep, however sexy her body was, then she was barking up the wrong tree, and he would enjoy telling her so in no uncertain terms. He should have guessed that she was all about flowers, chocolate and romance. He should have guessed it from the home-spun furnishings and the picture-postcard garden. She didn't know how the real world worked, but how could she, caught up in her own imaginary world of illustration, living in the middle of the countryside where life evolved at such a slower pace?

'It doesn't matter,' Heather said, starting somewhere in the middle, 'whether you fancy me or I fancy you.'

'And why would that be? I'm all ears. Because there's a higher plane somewhere? Some spiritual nirvana we should all be aiming for?' He had sat down on the sofa, legs crossed. She had switched on a couple of lamps and the room was bathed in a warm, mellow glow. The shadows made her look all the softer, more vulnerable, more unbearably feminine. He looked past her to the mantelpiece, which was cluttered with pictures in various size of frame. A hallmark of the incurable romantic, he thought cynically. There was no mantelpiece in his penthouse apartment and, if there had been, it certainly wouldn't have been groaning under the weight of photos.

'Because I used to be married!' There. It was out in the open now, and the silence that greeted her revelation was deafening. She could almost sense Leo's brutally sharp mind trying and failing to take it in.

'You were *married*?' he asked. He didn't know why he found that so shocking, but he did.

'To a man called Brian.' Having intended to leave out all

extraneous detail, Heather was now overcome with the urge to divulge every miserable second of her disillusioning experience. 'I… We were… I suppose you could say that we were childhood sweethearts. Went to the same secondary school, started going out when I was seventeen and he was eighteen, although we'd known each other long before then. Grew up together, you might say.'

Leo had said, in a voice that had been thick with sarcasm, that he was going to be all ears, that he couldn't wait to hear what she had to say. He hadn't expected this.

'You were married,' he repeated slowly.

'Yes. Haven't I just told you that?'

'I'm finding it hard to take in.'

'Why?' Because, she thought, he didn't think she really had what it took to get a guy for keeps? 'No, scrap that.'

'Because a husband isn't usually something most women keep to themselves, even husbands who are no longer on the scene.' He didn't add that most divorced women were fond of getting the sympathy vote and complaining about husbands who had left them high and dry—or maybe that was just his cynicism speaking, having been out with a couple of divorcees in the past, neither of which had lasted longer than three months apiece. Who wanted to spend what little free time they had listening to a woman ranting about her ex? 'Where is he now?' Leo asked.

He was already envisaging the type of guy she might have married, working out why she was so keen on fighting him. Once bitten, twice shy.

'In Hong Kong, as a matter of fact.'

'Hong Kong? What the hell is your ex-husband doing in Hong Kong?'

'You're amazed that I was married. You're amazed that my

ex-husband lives in Hong Kong. You don't have a very high opinion of me, do you?' Heather asked coldly, although there were tears just below the surface. She was remembering how she had failed to fit in to city life. The higher Brian had climbed, the more she had been left behind. She just hadn't been the right sort of woman. Why on earth was she feeling hurt because Leo was finding it hard to believe that she might ever have had a life outside the country cottage and the gardening interests?

'It has nothing to do with whether or not I have a high opinion of you.' *Married? Hong Kong?* He had managed to swallow his stupefaction that the woman had an ex in tow; had rapidly concluded that the hapless guy, the teenage sweetheart, must have been a country lad, had done whatever country lads did for a living—sheep farming, possibly—Heather would have become bored with him, with the monotony of being a farmer's wife... The familiar story of two lives drifting apart.

Sheep farmers, however, did not usually emigrate to Hong Kong.

'You portrayed yourself in a certain light,' Leo told her evenly. 'I took you at face value. You never once mentioned that you were married. You don't wear a wedding ring. Believe it or not, my immediate conclusion wasn't that you were a divorcee. Get where I'm going with this? If you can find the insult there, then please point it out.'

'You think that this—' she spread her arms wide to encompass everything inside the cottage and outside it '—is the sum total of my life? Is that why you figured that I was a safe bet to entice into bed with you—because I was so *backward* that I would be grateful and excited that a man like you, a man of the world, might condescend to show some interest in me?

Interest of a passing nature, of course—because, as you've told me, you're not into permanence. Not that I wouldn't have guessed that.'

Leo recalled his ready expectations that the attraction between them would result in bed and had the grace to flush.

'No one could accuse you of being backward,' he muttered grimly.

Heather looked at him with fierce, angry eyes. It would have been helpful if she could have superimposed Brian's face onto his, but no such luck. All she could see was his stupendous beauty, the lithe muscularity of his body. It made her more determined to have her say, to make sure that he knew in no uncertain terms that she wasn't up for grabs. That way, he would avoid her as much as she was desperate for him to. She didn't want to constantly feel fearful that she might just bump into him. She didn't want to be tempted.

His expression was still and watchful. For a couple of seconds, her imagination took flight, and she wondered where they would be now if she had never said anything, if she had given in to that kiss completely and had let it take her to the step beyond. They would be upstairs in her king-sized bed. They would be naked and entwined, and she would be burning up with lust.

She closed her eyes briefly, feeling faint. She had to make a big effort to remind herself that a bit of pleasure would never be worth the loss of her self-esteem, which had taken such a long time to reconstruct.

'How long have you been divorced?'

Heather opened her eyes and inhaled deeply. 'A couple of years.'

'What happened?' Did this qualify as drama? Leo didn't know. He just knew that he wanted her to finish whatever it was she had to say. If only, he told himself, so that he could walk away and thank his lucky stars for his near escape. A woman with baggage was never worth the hassle.

Besides, he still hadn't found out what the sheep farmer was doing on the other side of the world.

'What happened was that I married a guy who ended up making money his god.'

'Not following you. What did you say he did?'

'He was an investment banker. In the city. So, you see? I'm not quite the rustic country-bumpkin you thought I was.'

Like a jigsaw puzzle, the pieces were now slotting together at mind-boggling speed. So that was why she had been so knowledgeable about financial matters; why she had been so wary and distrustful of him. Did she think that she could just stand there and make comparisons?

Leo didn't know the guy, but he was outraged that he should be compared to anyone.

'Investment banker. Hence your knowledge of the stock market.'

'Oh yes,' Heather said bitterly. 'There was a time when I knew everything there was to know about what was happening in the world of high finance.' Her eyes glazed over. She forgot that Leo was there. 'You see, I thought that if I took an interest in what he did, I mean *really* took an interest, then he might be able to see that I was more than just the teenager who came from his home town. So I read up on all that stuff, even though it bored me to death.'

Leo, listening intently, could pick up on the hurt lying just below the surface, and he felt an irrational desire to find this character and knock him into kingdom come.

''Course, it didn't work.' Heather refocused on Leo. If he had tried interrupting her, asking questions, then she might have abbreviated everything, but his silence was the equivalent of a key unlocking a box. She hadn't poured her heart out to anyone, and a part of her was stunned that she should choose to do so now with the most unlikely of candidates. But then it wasn't as though she risked seeing him again. People bared their souls to their hairdressers, didn't they? It was the same sort of thing, wasn't it?

'He was in less and less. How could I show off my knowledge of all things financial if he just wasn't around?'

'How old were you?'

'Nineteen. Too young and too impressionable to see what was staring me in the face.'

'He moved on,' Leo said flatly, and she gave an imperceptible nod.

'He was talented. A whizz kid. There was a whole list of "youngest ever" records which he'd broken, as he kept telling me. He had to work all hours, he also kept telling me, and fool that I was I accepted it. I busied myself with my art course and dashed back in the evenings to make meals that ended up in the bin most of the time.' She glanced quickly at Leo but she couldn't read what he was thinking. She had come so far with the sorry recital that there seemed little point in cutting it short now. And, besides, it was cathartic, spilling her guts.

'I guess I knew it was all coming to an end, but I still hung on like an idiot until I got a call from an anonymous woman telling me that she was having an affair with my husband. She'd just been ditched in favour of a newer model, and I guess she decided that telling me was the best revenge she could have. 'Course, I confronted Brian and, needless to say, he didn't deny it. I think he was relieved, in a way.'

Watching her face was like watching a slideshow of emotions.

He realised that he was clenching his fists and he slowly breathed out, unclenched them, and waited for her to continue.

'You see, he was ashamed of me.' Heather held her chin up and looked Leo squarely in the face. 'Wrong clothes, wrong hair, not polished enough. The more money he earned, and the richer he became, the more his tastes changed. He no longer wanted small and plump and curly haired, he wanted leggy and blonde. Models. He was sorry, of course. And guilty too. He offered me as much money as I wanted, but all I took was enough to buy this cottage so that I could have a safe roof over my head while I kick-started my career back here. I didn't know whether I'd find work or not, but it was a relief not to have to worry about meeting a mortgage while I looked. He got a transfer to Hong Kong, and good luck to him. As far as I'm concerned, he sold his soul to the Devil.'

'And you've decided that I'm cut from the same cloth as a man who turned out to be an irresponsible philanderer.'

Put like that, Heather was uncomfortably aware that she might have been a bit liberal with her comparisons. But, when you looked at the bigger picture, weren't they more or less the same—rich men who thought that they could buy whatever and whoever they wanted to? That their wealth entitled them to walk all over people without any regard to feelings? Leo and his 'here today, gone tomorrow' women were only a hop and a skip away from Brian and his 'out with the old, in with the new', weren't they? Okay, so there might be some inconsistencies in the detail, but if you got bogged down in the detail, then you were lost.

She shrugged.

'You were more than willing to use me,' Heather began, but she faltered when she saw the thunderous, enraged expression on his face.

'Use you? *Use you?*'

'You think you can have whatever you want.'

'You're an adult. I'm an adult. As far as I'm concerned, sex between two consenting adults doesn't involve exploitation of any kind, and believe me, I don't need to coerce a woman into my bed. Your ex-husband may not have turned out to be the man you thought he was, but don't even think of lumping me in the same category.'

'You can't deny that you're cocooned by your wealth.' Heather was angry that he was trying to trip her up, trying to use clever words to make her feel as though she had made a mistake about him. She hadn't!

'I don't use it as an excuse to get women,' he grated. 'And that's a despicable insinuation. Have I tried to buy you with gifts, in any way?'

'No, but—'

'But *what*? Are you going to eliminate every man from your life whose name begins with the letter B?' he asked, his mouth twisting cynically. 'Maybe it might just be safer to eliminate all men from your life. Then you can be guaranteed never to be hurt again.' He stood up and noticed the way she cringed back, as though he posed some kind of physical threat to her. That was even more of a red rag as far as he was concerned.

'Don't worry,' he said scathingly. 'I won't come near you.'

On his way to the door, Leo paused and turned to her. 'An empty bed is a lonely place,' he said coolly.

'Better empty than littered with all the wrong kind of guys,' Heather threw back at him. Her eyes were stinging. She knew that as soon as he left she was going to cry, because she could feel the tears pricking against her eyelids.

Leo swore softly under his breath. He should never have

given in to this attraction, should never have seen her as a challenge. Challenge? The woman was more than a challenge! Had he forgotten how many thorns a rose could have? Damn it, the woman would have a hell of a time finding any man who wouldn't run a mile in the face of that tongue of hers!

The fact that she was standing there, looking as though she would collapse like a rag doll the minute her strings were cut, was no concern of his. She had said what she wanted to say, wrapped up in the greatest insults possible, and he didn't have time for this.

'*You* had a bad marriage,' she said tightly. 'And the way you deal with it is by never getting close to anyone. You don't want any woman to penetrate your fortress, so you just have affairs—nothing permanent, nothing that could get too emotionally messy.'

'Spare me the analysis.'

'Because that's something else you're *not into*? There are quite a few things you're *not into*, aren't there?' Her skin felt hot and tight. She knew in some part of her that was still being rational that there was no need for her to start having a go at him, but she wanted to. She was just so angry that she had allowed herself to get in this situation in the first place.

'I may have that lonely bed for a while, but at least I won't be scarred for ever. At least I know that there's someone out there who's right for me, and I know that someone isn't going to be a workaholic who doesn't have time for the rest of the human race!'

'This conversation,' Leo drawled, stepping out of the door and reaching for his car keys in his pocket, 'is officially closed.'

Heather watched as he let himself out of the room, out of the front door, out of her orbit. Success; she had said her piece. He wouldn't try anything again.

She should have been sagging with relief.

Instead, she felt one tear dribble down her cheek, followed by another, as she contemplated the lonely bed waiting for her upstairs.

CHAPTER FIVE

AT TEN past nine on a Wednesday evening, Leo finally allowed himself to scan through the last of his emails, and swivelled his chair round so that he could stare at the uninterrupted view of skyline from his London office.

Like his apartment, his office was cool, uncluttered and furnished in the kind of uber-modern style that only real money could buy. One white wall was dominated by an abstract painting, subject incomprehensible. The carpet was pale and thick, and the furniture was a light, solid wood, handmade to stand the test of time, with very clever drawers that opened and closed without the benefit of handles. Leo had left it all to his design team and was still pleased with the result after five years. He could have had it stripped and updated but what would have been the point? He would still have gone for something similar.

A working environment should not indulge in the luxury of distractions.

And his private life should likewise be uncomplicated.

He frowned, very much aware that, since Heather Of The Background Issues had burst into his life a month previously, his private life had been anything but uncomplicated.

And this despite the fact that he hadn't set eyes on her since their last encounter.

Twice he had visited his mother and Daniel, even staying for the whole weekend, which he seldom did, as time was a commodity rarely at his disposal. On both occasions, Heather had been conspicuous by her absence. She was clearly avoiding him at all costs. After some casual questioning he had discovered, via Daniel and his mother separately, that she had variously been away on an art course or visiting friends up north.

'Busy lady,' he had remarked, at which point he had been subjected to an enthusiastic account of her good work in the community by his mother—art classes for the little kids; volunteer work helping with the gardens once a month at the local retirement homes; cake baking, apparently, whenever there was a cake to be baked.

'But no guy in her life,' he had murmured encouragingly. 'All that domestic stuff probably makes them run a mile.' Having taken minimal interest in the doings of the various people in his mother's life, a habit born over time and cemented through the years, he had been amused to find himself assaulted with all the tittle tattle that seemed to comprise village life.

His mother had even tentatively suggested, without prompting, two visits to London, and had arrived with Daniel clutching a London guide with pages marked at various places they wanted to visit. Gone were the expensive meals out and in had come sightseeing on a major scale. Leo had found, close and personal, queues, cafés and tourist sights he had never clapped eyes on.

Now, staring out of his window, he cursed himself for the fact that he couldn't stop thinking about Heather. He had left her house weeks ago and had convinced himself that he had

had a lucky escape. If she wanted to nurse her bitterness and bury herself in a solitary existence pretending that she was happy, then that was her affair. He wasn't in the business of trying to persuade her otherwise. In fact, he wasn't in the business of trying to persuade *any* woman into bed with him. He never had been, and he wasn't about to start now.

It irked him, however, that she was still managing to fester away inside some corner of his brain, disrupting the smooth running of his life, causing him to lose concentration in the middle of meetings. Even when he had been out with one of his lawyer friends, a glamorous blonde whom he had dated off and on in the past, he had still been unable to shake off the uninvited image of another woman—one with curly, golden hair and soft, blue eyes—adorning his bed.

Never having dealt with a woman walking away from him, Leo could only think that his problem lay in the novelty of the situation in which he now found himself.

Why else would she still be on his mind, like a low-level virus he hadn't quite managed to clear out of his system?

Or maybe, having bought into the notion that he needed to have a change from clever, hard-nosed power babes, he was just frustrated at having his plans thwarted.

Leo was unaccustomed to analysing emotional situations. The women he had dated in the past had seldom brought their personal baggage to the table, and the ones who had had been the quickest to go. That was just the way he operated and he was unapologetic about it. Now he found himself spending far too much time thinking about what Heather had said, furious at her self-righteous assumption that she was somehow morally superior to him because she had decided on a life of self-imposed celibacy to deal with what had obviously been a grim marriage.

He was scowling, chewing over her accusations that he was little more than a ruthless womaniser, when he felt the vibration of his mobile phone in his pocket.

His first thought was that he hoped it wasn't the leggy, blonde lawyer. They had parted company without having made any arrangements to meet up again, but she had threatened to be 'in touch', and he had been too polite to tell her not to bother.

He therefore answered in the tone of voice of someone prepared to deliver a let down.

To hear Heather's voice down the line brought him to his feet in surprise, but he recovered fast and bypassed all the usual pleasantries to ask curtly what she wanted.

His response was pretty much what she had expected, but, hearing his dark, velvety voice at the other end of the line, still had Heather's nerves jangling.

She had steeled herself to make the call, had known that she had to. In her hand, she was still clutching Katherine's address book, which she had found in the little chest of drawers by the telephone in the kitchen as instructed.

'I'm sorry to disturb you,' she apologised. 'I tried your land line at your house, but you weren't in.'

'Repeat. What do you want?'

'There's no need to be so hostile.'

'You've interrupted me in the middle of…let's just say I'm busy.'

Busy doing what? Heather thought. *And with whom?* She swallowed back a dark, intrusive jealousy that sprang out at her from nowhere and left her shaken.

'It's about your mother.'

Leo tensed. 'What about my mother?'

'She's in hospital,' Heather told him bluntly.

'*Hospital?* That's impossible. I spoke to her last night and she was perfectly fine.'

'She's had a fall, Leo. She was using the ladder to change a light bulb and she fell. Apparently she hadn't secured it properly, and she must have landed in an awkward position. Daniel and I have just come back from the hospital. She's broken her leg, and I'm afraid she's going to be there for at least a couple of weeks. I'm sorry. I know you're all wrapped up with you whatever it is you're in the middle of doing, but you're going to have to come up.'

'I'm on my way.'

So this was how it felt to have someone hang up on you. She took a couple of seconds to regain her composure, then she turned to Daniel, who was exhausted and finishing the last of the meal which she had hurriedly prepared for him the minute they had set foot back into the house.

'Your dad's on his way here,' she said with a reassuring smile. Daniel hadn't reacted well to his grandmother's fall, and Heather suspected that it was because she had become the one stable person in his life, the adult on whom he had learnt to depend following his mother's death. The ambulance, that ride to the hospital, seeing Katherine's ashen face, must have taken him back in time. Heather had made sure to be very gentle with him and to assure him that everything was going to be just fine. She had brought him home, sat him down at the kitchen table and made him a fluffy cheese-omelette with potatoes and chatted comfortingly about inconsequential things that had happened to him at school.

'When you've finished eating I'll run you a nice, hot bath, and then it's sleep time for you, Dan.'

'Do I have to go to school tomorrow? I haven't done my homework.'

'Oh, I think Miss Porter will understand. I'll take you in and explain the situation myself, so there's no need for you to worry on that score.' She began clearing away his dishes, stacking them in the dishwasher.

'Will my father be here when I get up in the morning?'

'Of course he will!' Just the thought of Leo closing the gap between them in that big, silent car of his was enough to bring her out in a cold sweat. She had been careful to avoid being around on the occasions he had visited. Yes, avoidance was always the coward's way of dealing with a problem, but Heather hadn't cared. If thinking about the man had sent her nerves into crazy free fall, then how bad would it have been to actually see him? Worse, to have to *talk* to him and feel those fabulous eyes of his rake over her with pity and scorn? Because she knew without a shadow of a doubt that he would not have understood a word of what she had told him about learning from her past experience with Brian, about not jumping into bed with anyone just because she happened to fancy them. He had looked at her as if she had taken leave of her senses, and she had been left feeling like Miss Haversham on a bad day.

'He's your dad, Daniel,' Heather asserted with more optimism than confidence. 'He's going to be here when you need him.'

'He can't be here. He works in London. He showed me around his office the last time we went down. He says he's away a lot. What if he's away and Gran's still in hospital? What then?'

'He runs his own company, Dan. He can choose whether he goes away or not, and if he's needed here then he'll *choose* to stay put.'

That closed that particular line of enquiry, and Heather didn't show how anxious she was that Daniel's predictions did not materialise. Katherine had been thrilled with what she had described as her son 'making such a big effort', but as far as Heather was concerned Leo's 'big effort' was only *really* big in comparison to how extremely *small* it had been before. With Katherine in hospital, Leo would have to make more than just what he considered 'a big effort'. He would have to put great sections of his life on hold.

The little boy fell into sleep within minutes and, without the distraction of his worrying list of questions, Heather had time on her hands to get really wound up over Leo's impending arrival.

She felt crumpled and unprepared. Three hours previously, Katherine had called and calmly explained that she had taken a tumble from a step ladder and was in a little bit of pain. In fact, Heather had rushed over to find the older woman on the ground, unable to move and white as a sheet. There had only been time to phone for an ambulance, to try to comfort a wide-eyed, terrified Daniel, and then the mad, panicked hospital scenario of waiting and X-rays and doctors. Any question of having a bath had been out of the question, and so here she was, dishevelled and unable to leave the house, because Daniel was upstairs sleeping and couldn't be left on his own.

She calmed herself with a pot of tea, having phoned the hospital and spoken to Katherine, who was sorted out in a private room, and thankfully in considerably less pain, but anxious about Daniel and about having to go under the knife.

She must have fallen into a light doze because the sharp ring of the doorbell made her jump and she hurried out, giving herself no time to dwell on the prospect of seeing Leo again and thereby get herself into a tizzy.

She had managed to convince herself that he couldn't be as impossibly overwhelming as she remembered, that his impact had really only been so powerful because initially she had not expected him to be so good-looking; that she had had valuable time to put everything into perspective and so would be prepared to face him. Besides, none of that mattered, given the situation.

She was wrong on all counts.

She pulled open the door and momentarily froze. Her skin suddenly felt hot and tight and she had a moment of sheer, blind panic as she took in the stunningly beautiful lines of his lean, chiselled face; she was as much affected by his masculine beauty now as she had been the first time she had clapped eyes on him. Against her lacy bra, she could feel her nipples tingle and harden and respond to that unbidden memory that this was the man who had wanted to make love to her.

'Are you going to stand there gaping for much longer?' Leo asked. He placed the palm of his hand flat against the door and gave it a little push, which was Heather's cue to step back immediately and rein in her turbulent thoughts.

He had noticed her gaping at him like a teenager with a crush! She could have died of embarrassment.

'You made good time,' she said, clearing her throat.

'No traffic at this time of night.' Leo strode into the house and then turned around to look at her. 'Tell me what happened. In detail.'

'Of course. Would you like something to drink?' She watched in fascination as he impatiently began rolling up the sleeves of his white shirt. He had ditched the tie at some point during the journey, and her eyes were drawn to that slither of bronzed skin where the top two buttons of his shirt had been undone.

'Just tell me what happened, and then I intend to head straight to the hospital.'

'Now?'

'I'm not one to stand around waiting for the grass to grow under my feet.'

'But no one's going to be there! I mean of course, your mother will be there, but you won't be able to find a doctor or anything.'

'You'd be surprised what I'm capable of achieving,' Leo informed her with such bone-deep, casual conviction that Heather was left in no doubt that he would have a consultant dashing out to see him at the speed of light.

He was heading towards the kitchen and Heather followed in his wake, rather like an obedient dog waiting to take orders from its master. As he grabbed himself a bottle of water from the fridge and began to drink, he actually snapped his fingers, and she began telling him the sequence of events, concluding by assuring him that his mother was fine, all things considered.

Leo continued to drink until the water was completely gone, then he looked at her carefully.

He had been looking forward to seeing her again, having, with a sense of satisfaction, regained control over the situation by realising that her vanishing acts had been a direct consequence of the impact he had made on her—forget all that rubbish about never going near a man like him in a thousand years. If she had been so convinced of her rightness, she wouldn't have spent the two weekends he had been up on mysterious away-days.

Of course, he wouldn't touch her with a barge pole now, but it still made him feel good that he hadn't been off-target when he had tuned in to that high-voltage sexual awareness he had felt emanating from her.

Annoyingly, however, he was aware that his body was lagging behind his thoughts for once.

Not even the alarming dullness of her clothes—a pair of

baggy, grey jogging-bottoms, an equally baggy tee shirt and an even baggier cardigan thrown over it—could reduce the surge of adrenaline he had felt the minute she had opened the door to him.

The fact that she hadn't been able to conceal her reaction to seeing him was overshadowed by the realisation that he wasn't quite as much in control of things as he had anticipated.

'Why didn't you think to call me sooner?'

Heather counted to ten. 'Everything was frantic here. By the time things had calmed down and Katherine had been seen to, I called you at your house, but you weren't there and your mother couldn't remember your mobile number.'

'It's programmed into her phone.'

'Which she didn't think to take with her!' She took a deep breath.

'She must have asked you to bring it for her once she was at hospital?'

'Katherine doesn't see her mobile phone as some kind of indispensable appendage, Leo. *You* might, but she doesn't. In fact, she very rarely remembers to take it with her when she goes out so, no, it wasn't on her list of requests when I came back here to fetch her some clothes for the hospital. If I had seen it lying around, then I might have thought to take it in for her, but I didn't.'

'And I suppose it didn't occur to you to look for it because it's not a *necessary appendage* for you either?' He raked his fingers through his hair in frustration because he could feel himself getting away from the matter in hand, falling victim to an inexplicable surge of something, some uninvited emotion that he didn't want or have time for. 'I might have got here sooner if I had been contacted earlier. How's Daniel been?'

'How do you think?' Heather asked, and then she subdued

her aggression to add, in a more level voice, 'He's been pretty rotten, poor kid. I think he remembers… Well, it might help if you talk to him. He's asleep now, but in the morning. Just reassure him that everything's going to be okay.'

'Of course.' How the hell was he going to do that? Leo wondered. That kind of intimate conversation with his son did not come naturally to him. Maybe, if he'd been a father figure throughout his formative years, he might know how to handle things… But, no; he refused to think of the unpleasant circumstances surrounding that murky issue. In the past month or so, the boy had at least begun to look at him slightly less unforgivingly. He had opened up enough to occasionally mention his mother, but there had been no heart-to-heart chats about feelings and emotions. How was he supposed to handle that now? 'I expect this must bring back memories,' Leo said, annoyed to realise that he was looking for clues on how to deal with the situation.

'Yes. I think so.' Some of Heather's tension melted away. 'He might need a bit of reassurance that you aren't going to disappear with Katherine in hospital.'

'Disappear?'

'As in hot foot it back to London the minute you have a quick word with the consultant.'

In truth, the reality of the situation was really only now beginning to sink in. His mother would be off her feet for some weeks. He would have to make suitable arrangements for Daniel. He could hardly be expected to abandon work for an indefinite period of time; it had been years since he had taken more than a few days off!

'Right. Well, I'm going to head off to the hospital now. I take it you will be able to cover here until I return?'

The underlying assumption was that she would be. Here

was a man who took it as a given that other people would have
no problem in falling in with whatever plans he had for them,
even if it meant disrupting their lives.

'Yes, but then I'll need to be away.'

'Naturally. Art courses to attend, friends to visit.'

'How did you know about the art course?'

Leo decided that it was definitely time to go. 'My mother
must have said something in passing.' He began walking away.
It was late, and it would probably have been more sensible to
wait until morning before going to the hospital, but something
had changed between his mother and him over the past weeks.
Having been emotionally independent of her for more years
than he cared to remember, Leo had recently made tentative
steps to bridge the invisible gap that separated them. He had
stepped out of his cocoon and begun to see the considerable
sacrifices which she had made for him with Daniel. He had
also been treated to one or two trips down memory lane,
which was a place he had seldom visited, and had begun
piecing together a past that might not have been quite as clear
cut as he remembered.

Now, he was reluctant to jeopardise that fragile relationship by showing up in his own sweet time, allowing his
mother to assume, with that resigned air of hers, that yet again
the pressing demands of work took precedence over everything else.

'What time do you think you'll be back?' Heather pressed
him for an answer.

'Couple of hours. Why?'

'Look at me!' She drew his attention to her dishevelled
state and then instantly regretted it when he paused to look at
her. It was a thorough inspection that took in the very worst
of her stay-at-home gear, the sort of clothes which would

have had her instantly hanged, drawn and quartered by the Fashion Police. She hadn't glanced into a mirror recently, but she was willing to bet that her face was shiny and her hair was a mop. 'I need a bath,' she muttered.

'I don't remember telling you that you couldn't have one.' Leo shrugged, gritting his teeth as his imagination surged beyond her unsightly garb to the body underneath. 'I have a wardrobe of spare clothes upstairs. Feel free to take what you need.'

Heather could think of nothing she would rather do less, but she nodded, willing him on his way so that she could take advantage of his absence to shower, change and scramble into one of the five spare bedrooms before he returned.

Thanks to an interruption by Daniel, who had woken and had needed comforting and then a rambling story before he fell back to sleep, it was nearly midnight by the time Heather had her much-longed-for bath. She found one of Leo's pristine white work-shirts to use as a nightie. Although it was much shorter than anything she usually dared wear, at least it was clean.

Having had nothing to eat for the evening, she was aware of the growling pains in her stomach when she finally settled into bed and turned off the light. Her last meal had been hours previously, a snatched sandwich in between preparing some stuff for the art class which she did at the local school.

Now, with her stomach noisily reminding her of that fact, she tiptoed out of the bedroom, down the majestic winding staircase and into the kitchen.

The house was in darkness save for the light in the hall. Leo still hadn't returned, or if he had he had managed to make absolutely no noise. Since he didn't strike her as the kind of thoughtful guy who would tiptoe through the house in darkness rather than wake its sleeping occupants, Heather assumed that he had become caught up in the sluggish hospital system and was probably tearing his hair out while he waited for people to do his bidding.

She was inspecting the contents of the fridge, and indulging in a pleasant daydream of the great man undone by a hospital system which refused to do as it was told, when she was aware of a sound behind her.

She spun around, armed with nothing but a bar of chocolate, and her eyes widened at the sight of Leo lounging against the kitchen door, eyebrows raised in an amused question.

'You're back.'

'So it would seem.' His gaze was shuttered as he looked at her, standing in front of him like a rabbit caught in the headlights, and wearing one of his shirts, something which he found unaccountably appealing. It was buttoned tight across her fabulous body and her breasts spilled beyond the confines of the thin fabric, revealing a generous cleavage and an eyeful of her circular, pouting nipples pressed darkly against the cotton. He quickly refocused on her face, now tinged pink with embarrassment, although she seemed unaware that the nightdress left precious little to the imagination.

'I… I was just getting myself something to eat… I haven't had anything today, what with one thing and another…'

'And all you've found is a bar of chocolate?' Leo was finding it hard not to stare. The woman had the body of a sex siren, with the sort of generous curves that were the stuff of most teenage boys' fantasies. He strode into the kitchen and watched out of the corner of his eye as she fell back onto one of the kitchen chairs, chocolate still in hand. 'I'll make you something to eat. Chocolate's just going to send a sugar rush through you, and you'll have to kiss sweet goodbye to getting any sleep.' He pulled out some eggs and cracked them into a bowl.

'There's no need for you to do this.' Heather was now painfully aware that she was being a chore on top of everything else. 'I've lost my appetite anyway.'

'No, you haven't,' Leo informed her. 'You're just embarrassed at being caught red-handed in the kitchen. At any rate, you need to keep your strength up.'

'What are you talking about?' When that failed to get a response, she added nastily, 'I thought you didn't do Mr Domestic.'

'I think I'm on safe territory with you. Eggs—scrambled or fried?'

'Scrambled would be fine. Thank you.' Of course he was on safe territory! She was history, as far as he was concerned. There was now some other sucker in his life. No; Heather was definitely *not* going to think about that. 'How is Katherine? Did you get to see her? Talk to her? Or was she asleep?'

'Yes, to the first two. Surprisingly awake, considering the time, but she tells me that she has trouble falling asleep. First I knew of that.' He began stirring the eggs in the frying pan, and put bread in the toaster.

'She must have been really pleased to see you. And the doctor—did you manage to get hold of one?' She could feel herself rambling and made an effort to stop, to act normally.

'Of course I did,' he said, sounding surprised that she had ever doubted that he would. 'It's all straightforward, but the healing time might run into weeks.' He tipped the egg onto the slice of toast on a plate and placed it in front of her. And without missing a beat he added, 'Which is where you come in.'

It took a few seconds for that postscript to sink in because she was busy losing herself in the fluffy perfection of the plate of food in front of her. She had never been heavily into meal-skipping.

'What?' She glanced across the table to where he had taken up position on the chair facing her.

'How's the egg?'

'Delicious. What did you say just then?'

'Finish eating and then we'll discuss it.' He noticed she didn't fiddle with her food, shoving it around her plate as if trying to distance herself from what she was eating. She dug in. He found that he liked that, or at any rate it made a pleasant change. Even power babes, intelligent enough to know better, were usually trapped by their own vanity and desire not to put on weight. The slice of toast would have been avoided like the plague.

'Discuss what?' She could have eaten the lot all over again. She felt calmer now, protected by the comforting width of the kitchen table. Being surprised by him like that had threatened to turn her into a dithering wreck, but she had taken her cue from him. They were just a couple of people discussing an unexpected situation. The fact that his presence did something to her peace of mind was neither here nor there.

'Ah...' Leo stood up and cleared away the plate, now scraped clean. 'My mother is going to need someone around while she's in hospital, and quite possibly when she gets out.'

'Yes. She will.' Heather challenged him with her direct gaze. 'And so will Daniel.'

'And I will be here, as much as I can. But when I am not...'

'You want me to cover for you.' She bristled with anger and with a certain amount of weird disappointment. 'Is that why you told me that I needed to keep my strength up? Why you decided to spend five minutes pretending to be thoughtful, whipping me up some scrambled eggs on toast?' That hurt. 'Katherine in hospital, and me bed ridden with flu because I haven't eaten, just wouldn't do, would it? Because nothing can be allowed to get in the way of work, can it?' She stood up abruptly and began to walk towards the door, only to turn around and find him virtually on top of her.

'This argument is beginning to get a little tired, Heather.' He took hold of her arm, and when she tried to shake him off held her a little harder, then he sighed and released her with an impatient shake of his head. He said heavily, 'I'm going to try to be around as much as I possibly can, but inevitably there will be times when I physically can't be.'

Reluctantly, Heather conceded that he was being realistic. 'I just don't like being manipulated,' she told him tightly, at which he flung back his head and gave a roar of laughter.

'You? *Manipulated?* Not a word that I would associate with you. If you don't feel that you have the time or the inclination to help me out here, then I will get my personal assistant to house sit as necessary when I can't be around. Naturally, Joanna wouldn't be my first choice, because you are familiar with Daniel and I am reluctant to introduce him to a stranger, but the choice is yours.'

It was a choice in name only, she acknowledged, but she wasn't going to cave in to his demands without laying down a few conditions of her own.

Before she could open her mouth, he added, 'Naturally, I wouldn't expect you to do it for nothing. You will be compensated financially. However much you want.'

'In other words, you would become my employer, so to speak?'

Leo frowned, taken aback at having his generosity, as he saw it, thrown back in his face. And *this* was the woman who had caused him sleepless nights! Pay her a compliment, and she would fight like a wild cat to prove she had been insulted. Give her a bunch of flowers, and she would probably claw your eyes out! *Narrow escape*, he told himself again. *And, when you're busy fantasising about ripping off her clothes and losing yourself in that body of hers, just remember that the woman's a hell cat.* Nowhere was it written that having a relationship with a hell cat was the sort of calming experience a man needed.

'In *other words*, I would recognise that having your life disrupted might interfere with your work, ergo a lack of income. End of story.'

Deprived of that line of argument, Heather huffed and then said, 'Well, I wouldn't dream of charging you for being here with Daniel if you're not around—which isn't to say that you have carte blanche to pop in now and again whenever it happens to suit you. And another thing—no women.'

'Come again?'

'No women.'

'And why would that be?'

Heather's cheeks flamed. 'Because it would be disres—'

'Climb off your high horse! I wouldn't dream of bringing any women up here. But, as a matter of interest,' he added, 'would you be jealous? Because that's just the sort of condition a jealous woman might consider.' He laughed again, because now she looked fit to explode. Give her a second or two, and he would have to dodge some serious aerial bombardment from whatever heavy objects were to hand. He had been stressed out, but finally he was beginning to relax.

'You really need to sit down and have a chat with your ego, Leo. If you let me know when you're going to be away…'

'Let you know? My life isn't predictable like that. No, I have a much better idea. You move in, and that way we can both save ourselves a lot of trouble making phone calls or knocking on doors. That would seem the most sensible option, wouldn't you agree?'

CHAPTER SIX

LESS than thirty-six hours later, Heather was standing in the sprawling hall of Katherine's house, watching with her mouth open as Leo basically commandeered the place. The man hadn't been kidding when he had told her that he didn't let the grass grow under his feet. The house was teeming with people in uniforms who were efficiently doing all sorts of clever things to turn two of the downstairs rooms into offices. In the midst of this organised chaos, Leo was standing, mobile glued to his ear, giving hand commands to the men while he restlessly barked orders to some hapless soul on the other end of the line.

Heather had just come across to fetch some books for Katherine and a few changes of clothes, but she was transfixed by the scene unfolding in front of her.

Three men, bending under the weight of an enormous desk, jostled her from behind, and she let out a little yelp and side-stepped them.

Just then, Leo spotted her dithering by the front door and he snapped his mobile shut and headed in her direction.

Despite the cataclysmic changes to his routine, he was feeling pretty good. When he had told his mother that he would be moving into her house so that she need not worry about Daniel, he had been first surprised, then tickled pink by the exuberance of her gratitude. Daniel was his responsibility, after all, he had thought with a stab of guilt. How distant had he and his mother become that she would think that he might swoop in and out, leaving them all to muddle along the best they could? Notwithstanding, he had left the hospital feeling well disposed and in high spirits.

He had also, in an unprecedented U-turn, decided to change his plans. Instead of dipping in and out to the best of his ability, he would simply shift his working arena from London to his mother's house. He wouldn't be able to guarantee a one-hundred-percent attendance rate, but his movements would certainly be a little more predictable. He had felt good making that decision, and he felt good now, watching his stuff being shifted in, everything that would turn his mother's den and little snug into a working environment suitable for him.

Heather, he noticed, was gulping like a fish out of water and looking as though she had barged into a scene from a science fiction movie.

'What on earth is going on?' she gasped when he was virtually on top of her.

'What does it look like? I'm kitting out some work space for myself.'

And he wasn't above getting down and dirty in the process, she noted, taking in the low-slung, faded jeans and the tee shirt, likewise faded; he was displaying all the signs of a man sweating at some manual labour.

In fact, her nostrils quivered at his rough, masculine scent. Whoever said that aftershave was a turn on?

'You never said...' she stammered, and he raised his eyebrows sardonically.

'I didn't think I had to run it by you to get permission first.'

'That's not what I meant! I just hadn't expected that you would be moving in lock, stock and smoking barrel!' She watched in horror as he stripped off the tee shirt and tossed it across the oak banister. Sure, it was hot and sure, he was sweaty and looked as though he had been lifting a few heavy objects, but was that really necessary? She dragged her eyes away from the fascinating sight of his bare chest, bronzed and muscled, his nipples flat and brown. To look at him now, no one could ever accuse him of being a soft, desk-bound money maker. In fact, he looked like a man born into manual work, and extremely challenging manual work. There wasn't a spare ounce of flab on him. She cleared her throat nervously and pinned her eyes to his amused face.

'Does Katherine know that you're rearranging all her furniture?' she snapped in a high voice. Now she sounded like a school mistress—prim, proper, disapproving. *He* was supposed to be the buttoned-up businessman, and *she* was supposed to be the easygoing artist. When had this role reversal occurred? she wondered feverishly. 'I just thought that your presence here was going to be on a more casual basis, that's all.'

'I didn't think that *casual* would work, given the circumstances. Care to have a look at the furniture rearrangements while you're here? Then you can report back to my mother.'

'Of course I'm not going to report back to your mother!'

'No? It's just that you suddenly seemed ablaze with self-righteous zeal.'

Heather scowled as, amused, he turned his back on her and began walking towards what had been Katherine's snug and den. *Self-righteous zeal?* Not content with making her feel like Miss Haversham, he had now managed to reduce her to prissy schoolmarm with an overdeveloped streak of Puritanism.

And her body was still in a state of hyper-sensitivity at the sight of his semi-nudity.

Her legs unfroze from where they had been nailed to the floor and she tripped behind him, still scowling, to pull up short in front of a fully functioning office in progress. Ornaments, dainty bits of furniture, pot plants, all had been cleared away and replaced by modems, telephones, a fax machine and a small, flat-screen TV which constantly recorded the levels of the stock market. This was a male-dominated space now, and the dominating male was currently looking around him with an expression of satisfaction.

'What do you think?' Leo asked, spinning on his heels to face her. It was strange how much he enjoyed getting under her skin. Maybe it was pay back for her getting under *his* skin. And maybe there was an even bigger pay back to be had. Wouldn't it be nice, he thought as he watched her trying not to watch him, if her defences came crashing down even though she didn't want them to? Wouldn't it be satisfying if she found herself jumping from her moral high-ground even though her brain told her that she shouldn't?

The brain, after all, was a strange thing. You could go blue in the face telling it to do something and it would just head off at a tangent and go its own merry way. Wasn't that what had happened with him? He had sworn himself off her but, now that he was here, and that so was she, some inner devil he hadn't known he possessed was playing mind-games with him—and he liked these mind-games. Hadn't he always been big into sport, both of the intellectual and the physical variety?

Right now she was as stiff as a block of wood, and was making damned sure to look anywhere but at him.

'You're bristling.'

'I am *not* bristling.'

'My mother's stuff has been safely stored away in one of the other rooms. You can rest assured that I haven't started a bonfire with the lot. If you like, I can take you for an inspection, make sure I haven't broken anything in the moving process.'

'Ha, ha. Hilarious. Just out of interest, exactly how long are you planning to stay?' Heather asked, roaming round the room and inspecting all the new additions with a jaundiced eye. She could feel him behind her, all alpha-male temptation, which her disobedient fingers were longing to touch. She folded her arms just in case they developed a mind of their own.

'As long as it takes. Within reason, of course.'

'You've gone to all this expense for a few days?'

'*Days?* That's either a monumental understatement or a severe case of wishful thinking. I would think along the line of *weeks* rather than days.'

'All right, then. *Weeks.*'

'Time is money, and it pays for me to be able to work to a hundred-percent capacity while I'm here.'

'You've certainly done away with all the atmosphere,' Heather remarked, looking at the black ash-and-chrome desk festooned with high-tech equipment, so at odds with the faded, flowered wallpaper and the lonesome bowl of pot pourri on the bookcase which Leo had obviously missed by accident.

'It pays to have a working environment that's devoid of distractions.' No peculiar, baggy jogging-bottoms and oversized sweat shirt today. She was wearing a cotton dress with a pattern of very tiny flowers and a pair of sandals. He wondered, idly, exactly how long it would take him to undo the innumerable little pearl buttons that hooked her in.

He was vaguely aware that she was doing it again, making him lose focus, encouraging his rebellious mind to take a stroll down a pleasurable, imaginary path. Whereas before this had infuriated the hell out of him, Leo was fast losing interest in the urge to question the fact that the woman confused and confounded him like no other woman had ever done before.

Having always been a great believer in the inescapable truth that 'fate' was the last fallback of people who were too weak to realise that they controlled events, rather than the other way around, he was quite happy to put a different spin on things now. Fate had seen fit to throw them together, and who was he to deny his primal, manly urge to hunt and capture? He had tried bringing all his formidable intelligence and powers of reasoning to bear on the matter and what good had it done him? He had still ended up thinking of the woman way too much for his own good.

Logically, he deduced that if he could have her then he would be able to get her out of his system. Naturally, he would not be putting himself out to that end. It was all very well to rise above rejection, but he had his limits. No; she would come to him. *She* would surrender into his arms of her own volition. It would be a truly sweet surrender.

He surfaced to find her looking at him, at the tail end of something that had clearly been sarcastic, judging from the curl of her pink mouth.

'Sorry. Miles away. What did you say?'

Prissy, Heather thought, *self-righteous, zealous in all the wrong ways.* And now, to top it all, so boring that he had completely switched off from what she had been saying about liking distractions in the working environment.

'I was saying that I should get the clothes that I came for and then head for the hospital.'

'Give me half an hour. I'll take you.'

'There's no need, Leo...'

'No need for me to visit my mother?'

'You know that's not what I mean! You just seem to be very busy here.'

'Why don't you let me decide whether I can take time out or not? As you can see, I'm a big boy, more than capable of making decisions without a helping hand.'

Heather blushed furiously at the rebuke, but he wasn't looking at her. He was walking towards the door, pausing to discuss something with the guy who appeared to be in charge, then he turned to her.

'Why don't you go and do whatever it is you came here to do and meet me back in the hall in thirty minutes?'

'And why don't you stop giving orders?'

Leo shrugged and began making for the staircase. Heather was behind him. He could hear the soft tread of her steps above the noise of banging coming from the direction of the office. It was amazing how easy it was to rile her, he thought; not that that had been his intention. She was like a cat on a hot tin roof when she was around him, jumping at everything he said, bristling at hidden meanings to throwaway remarks, generally acting as though she would go up in smoke if he came too close to her.

'It's in my nature to give orders,' he said, not turning around. 'Why do you think that's a bad thing?'

'I'm surprised the people who work for you don't want you strung up! Don't you know that telling people what to do gets their back up?'

'Some people need telling what to do.' He made a right at the top of the staircase and was by his bedroom door when he finally turned to look at her. 'Besides, how else is a company supposed to be run unless there's someone in charge telling other people what to do? As a matter of fact, though, if you ask any of the people who work for me they'll tell you that I'm a pretty fair employer. Big bonuses, generous maternity and paternity leave, fantastic pension scheme… Nothing to complain about.' He leaned against the doorframe and stared down at her. 'Anyway,' he drawled, 'don't you think that some people actually *like* being told what to do?'

'No.'

'Because your ex made it his habit to tell *you* what to do?'

Heather flushed and then laughed derisively. 'Brian didn't tell me what to do. He just left me in the dark as to what *he* was up to. Anyway, that's not the point.'

Leo pushed himself away from the door frame and turned his back on her. 'You should loosen up,' he threw provocatively over his shoulder. 'You might find that life's less hard work when you're not continually arguing the finer points. In other words,' he added for good measure, 'you might actually *enjoy* being subservient…'

Heather was transfixed by the sight of him as he strolled towards his dressing table, leaning to support himself, hands flat on the polished wooden surface as he idly glanced down at the open laptop computer, then standing up, massaging his shoulder with one hand as he walked back towards her. The sound of his murmured, lazy voice was like a drug, making her thoughts sluggish and not giving her time to get herself all worked up by what he was saying.

'Subservient? I—I can't think of anything worse…' she stammered. She was having difficulty remembering what the original topic of conversation had been.

'No? Funny. Every woman I have ever known has ended up enjoying being controlled. Not in the boardroom, of course.'

He was standing right in front of her, and Heather took a couple of little steps back.

'Good for them.'

'You are not like them, however. That much I'll concede. But I guarantee there's one order I can give you that you'll jump to obey.'

'What?' she flung at him defiantly, her nerves skittering as he produced a wicked grin and reached for the zip on his jeans.

'Leave now or else watch me undress. I'm going to have a quick shower.'

Heather was out in two seconds flat. And in half an hour, during which the majority of Leo's extreme makeover appeared to have been completed, all bar the detail, she was standing at the door, still unnerved by that grinning last word he had had before she had fled the bedroom.

When he finally appeared, his hair was still damp and the jeans and sweaty tee shirt had been replaced with a pair of cream trousers and a cream shirt which made him look infuriatingly healthy and full of beans.

'I wasn't sure whether you would wait for me,' he said once they were on their way to the hospital. 'And if I embarrassed you back then, please accept my humble apologies.'

Heather looked at him suspiciously out of the corner of her eye. 'Contrite' wasn't an adjective she would have associated with him.

'You seem very nervous when you're around me—and I just want you to know,' Leo continued with a remorselessly pious voice, while he watched with fascination the transparent play of emotions on her face, 'that you have nothing to be afraid of.'

'Afraid? I'm not afraid.'

'No, maybe that's the wrong word. *Tense*. There's no need to feel tense when you're around me. Let's not lose sight of the main thing here, which is my mother. I see you're taking her a few books.'

Heather relaxed. Her imagination had gone into overdrive a bit earlier on, but she was coming back down to earth as she stared straight ahead and chatted to him about Katherine's progress. The operation had been a success, but she was still immobile and beginning to get bored. She was an avid reader, Heather said, hence the selection of books.

'She's particularly fond of travel books,' Heather told him. 'I think it makes her think of your brother, which is something I've been meaning to talk to you about.' With the busy hospital car-park now in sight, she was pleased with herself that she had managed to sustain a running conversation with Leo about nothing much in particular. There seemed to be a great black hole of missing information when it came to his mother, and he was either a very good actor or else he was genuinely interested in filling in some of the gaps which had hitherto existed.

'What about my brother?' Leo's mouth tightened but he kept his voice neutral.

'Do you know how to get in touch with him?'

'I fail to see where you're going with this.'

Heather glanced at him, surprised at the unwelcoming response. 'Don't you think that he should know about Katherine's fall?' This innocent question was greeted with stunning silence as Leo began driving slowly through the cluttered car-park, looking for a free space and complaining about the incompetence of the council, which had closed off a section of the car-park for repair work which appeared to be at a complete standstill.

'Aren't you going to give me a lecture about the virtues of public transport at this point?' he asked, neatly backing his car into a space which left them just about enough room to wriggle out. 'Or at least the perils of being seduced into buying cars that are too big to be useful? Maybe a sermon about the curse of the workaholic and the amount of time they waste trying to make money to buy things that aren't essential?'

After what had been a fraught-free drive to the hospital, Heather was confused at the sudden cool mockery in Leo's voice. Where had that come from?

'I don't care what you choose to spend your money on. It can't buy happiness.'

'There are times when you are a walking, breathing cliché, do you know that?'

'Why can't you be nice for longer than five seconds?' Heather snapped, glaring at him over the hood of his sleek car before slamming the door shut. 'One minute you're apologising for embarrassing me, and the next minute you're trying to start an argument for no good reason! I was just asking…'

'There's no need to drag my brother into this,' Leo told her abruptly, raking his fingers through his hair. 'Not that anyone is that certain of his whereabouts.'

'Your mother must know where he is,' Heather persisted. 'And wouldn't it be only fair to fill him in? Of course, if he's halfway across the world there's no need for him to head back to England, but he deserves to know.'

'This is not a matter open to discussion.'

'Your mother might disagree with that.'

Leo, striding towards the hospital entrance, swung round to face her.

She was staring up at him, hands planted firmly on her hips, her mouth pursed in angry defiance.

This was what turned him on and drove him nuts in equal measure. Driven by a sense of frustration, Leo reached out and pulled her angrily towards him, catching her by surprise so that she tumbled into him, her body soft and unresistant because she had had no time to shove him away.

There was nothing tender about the savage assault of his mouth against hers. He curled his long fingers into her hair and, although she was too stunned to put up much of a fight, he still drew her fiercely against him.

In that moment of complete shock, Heather felt her whole body go up in flames. It was as if a match had been struck inside her and had found that her defences, instead of being iron clad, were made of tinder.

Her lips parted wordlessly to accept his questing, urgent tongue. She heard herself give a soft moan. They were standing to one side, but she was still vaguely aware of people walking past them. Frankly, she couldn't have cared less what sort of spectacle they were making.

Her breasts were tender, crushed against his chest, and the abrasive rub of her bra against her nipples was sending tingling sensations all through her body, down to where a honeyed dampness had her aching for more.

When he tore himself away, it was like being hit suddenly by a cold breeze. She had a few seconds of realising that she actually missed having his arms around her. The silence between them seemed to stretch into eternity, and he wasn't looking at her. It didn't take the IQ of a genius to realise that he had come to his senses—which was more than she had done—and was already regretting his lapse in judgement.

'How dare you?' Heather struggled to hang on to her dignity, but her belated outrage withered away under his look of incredulity.

'Spare me the protest,' Leo told her. A group of people weaved around them and he pulled her further to one side. No, this was definitely *not* how things were supposed to happen. 'I didn't notice you turning away in revulsion. In fact, just the opposite— but then we both know what's going on here, don't we?'

'Yes! We're on our way to pay a visit to your mother and we—we made a bit of a mistake along the way…' She had the grace to blush. 'You kissed me, and…'

'You're going to have to stop doing that, you know.'

'Doing what?'

'Pretending that you're the innocent victim. It just doesn't sit well with the truth. Fact is, if we hadn't been here then there's no telling where we would have ended up.'

'Nowhere! I've already told you how I feel about you, how I feel about *relationships*.'

'I know. At great length. But it seems to me that your body's telling a different story.'

'I never said that I didn't find you an attractive specimen.' She liked the use of that word. It distanced her from the living, breathing, sexy, red-blooded male staring at her.

Leo cocked his head to one side and continued to look at her. In an ideal world—the one in which he played the starring role as the man destined to get precisely what he wanted and exactly in the manner in which he wanted it—there would have been dimmed lighting, an atmosphere of crackling, electric tension, the kind of tension that precedes inevitable surrender. She would have come to him, unable to resist her urges, melted into him and maybe, just maybe, he would have asked her to tell him just how much she wanted him.

Unfortunately the situation was hardly ideal. They were standing outside the hospital. There were people all around them, and the overhead sun was just about as far away from dimmed lighting as it was possible to get.

She also, crucially, had not come to him. She might not have been able to resist those urges of hers, but the stark truth of it was that she was backing away now at a rate of knots.

Leo was left wondering how the hell he had lost control of the situation yet again.

He had wanted to shut her up. The subject of his brother was off limits, and the desire to put it to rest had resulted in…

'Oh, I know that much,' he said softly. 'The little pretence you're hiding behind is that you can turn your attraction on and off like a tap.'

'We should go inside. Put that little lapse behind us.'

'Again.'

Heather flushed uncomfortably. *Again.* The softly spoken word dropped like a toxic rock into a still lake. She could feel the consequences rippling out.

'Okay. *Again.*' It took a lot of will power to meet his eyes when actually she wanted to duck inside the building and pretend that kiss had never taken place. *Again.*

'So what are you trying to say?'

'Nothing.' Leo shrugged and squinted against the sun. Twice he had felt the vibration of his mobile inside his pocket, twice he had chosen to ignore it. Playing truant definitely had its upside.

Although he was not looking at her—in fact, making sure not to look at her—he knew the female species intimately enough to know that this was a woman in the process of questioning herself, a woman on the edge of surrender, and the thought of that gave him an unbelievable high.

'Shall we go in? It's pretty hot out here.'

That was it, the sum total of his response?

Katherine was very upbeat, but for the entire time they were there Heather was unable to relax. Her eyes kept drifting to Leo—the way he sat, the way he crossed his legs, walked towards the window—everything.

By the time they finally left, she felt shattered. She had

meant to talk to Katherine about Alex, about whether she wanted him to know about the fall—because whether her son was told about the accident was her decision, and not Leo's—but in any event it never crossed her mind, which was far too busy thinking about other things.

It seemed ironic that when Leo had made that pass at her, had invited her into his bed, she had stoutly refused to have anything to do with the idea, had climbed onto her podium and made her feelings known loud and clear, had dispatched him with the ringing assertion that she was far too sensible to indulge in something for the wrong reasons.

She had just about managed to hold on to the notion that that one kiss had been an aberration.

This time, she knew what she had felt, and she knew that she had wanted much more. There was no way that she could hide behind the guise of the blushing fair maiden taken advantage of by the devil in disguise.

And now, Leo was far from interested in talking about anything. He might have kissed her, but it hadn't been a kiss of encouragement. He had been angry and frustrated with her, and his kiss had reflected that, it had been hard and punishing, and she had still clung to him like a limpet. She believed that she had actually moaned at one point.

'So...' she began hesitantly, once inside his car. 'Do you want to talk about what happened back then?'

Leo's brow knitted into a frown. 'What happened back then...?'

'You know.' He obviously had no idea what she was on about. 'You kissed me.'

'I thought we'd covered that subject.' Leo glanced across at her. 'Made a mistake, didn't make a mistake... There's just so much conversation two people can have on the subject of a kiss. We're not talking a national catastrophe here, Heather.'

She pursed her lips and stared straight ahead. Leo, focused on the road, couldn't see her expression, but he didn't have to. She had been thrown off-balance and this time she was finding it a little more difficult to dismiss. She couldn't duck and dive behind some phoney rubbish about being the horrified victim, and she couldn't even pretend that she had been caught off-guard and had therefore been the reluctant participant before coming to her senses. The lady had been his for the taking. But he wasn't going to indulge her very female need to discuss it to death, possibly to the point where she decided that flight, yet again, was the preferred response.

'No,' she said stiffly.

'We need to sort out the practicalities of what happens now,' he told her smoothly.

For a few seconds, Heather thought that he was talking about *them*. She felt a sickening lurch inside her as she realised that she wanted to talk about them, that she *wanted* to be persuaded to abandon every principle she had held dear for all these years, because her attraction to the wretched, inappropriate, totally unsuitable man was just too overwhelming.

When Heather had met Brian as a teenager she had been attracted to him, but it had been a girlish crush which had morphed over time into a relationship. Yes, she had always known that he was an attractive man, but she had never felt physically out of control when she had been around him. Leo did that to her. She didn't like it, but she could no longer deny it.

'Practicalities?' she asked faintly and he spared her another sidelong glance.

'Daniel?'

'Oh, right. Yes. Sure.' Heather sternly marshalled her

thoughts. 'Well, what's there to discuss? I mean, of course I'll be around if you need me at all, but I guess now that you've decided to adopt a hands-on approach to the situation it's pretty much sorted. Daniel sometimes trots over so that I can help him with some of his homework, and I don't mind that, especially if you're busy...'

'No can do.'

'I beg your pardon?'

'I've shifted my base, that's true, but my lifestyle is still going to be a little...erratic, shall we say?' They had cleared the town, and the open spaces around them seemed in harmony with his upbeat mood. It was odd, but in all his time coming here he had never really noticed his surroundings. Having always considered St James's Park to be the equivalent of the countryside, he was waking up to the reality that it was little more than a confined patch of green in the middle of a concrete jungle. So it was a pleasant eye-opener to be cruising along the winding little lanes, appreciating the scenery flashing past, not to mention the woman glowering in the seat next to him. That, likewise, was rather pleasant.

When he returned to the house, he knew that everything would be in place for him to slot neatly into an office that would be better equipped than most.

'Why should it be erratic?'

'Emergencies occasionally occur that require my presence. This afternoon, for example, I'm going to have to go to London to sort out some last-minute concerns from a small IT company I'm in the process of buying. Also, I may have set up camp in my mother's house, but that isn't to say that I'll be available for comment one hundred percent of the time. I would still like you to collect Daniel from school and feed him, by which time I will have done my utmost to make sure that my work's wrapped up for the evening. I know none of this is ideal for either of us, but it's for a limited period of time. Once it's over, we can both return to normality.'

'So you want me to spend the night at Katherine's?'

'If you don't mind?'

'No, that's fine.' While her head was still in a crazy spin, he, she couldn't help but notice, was as cool as a cucumber, super-polite and the last word in courteous. Heather was dismayed to find that she preferred the passion and heat of his anger.

'In fact,' Leo thought aloud, 'it might be altogether more convenient if you do as I've done—move in, just for a week or so. My mother should be back home by then, and I will get my housekeeper in London to come up and take care of all the chores as soon as she's back in the house. She'll need full-time help, and whilst Katrina's here she can also take care of the chores. She's an excellent cook in addition to everything else.'

A week or so… Temptation which would have had her bolting for cover a few weeks ago now dangled in front of her eyes like a banquet placed in front of a starving man. That second kiss had been a revelation. That little preaching voice that should have emerged and given her a strong lecture about keeping away from the man had gone into hiding, and in its place was a much more seductive voice, telling her that there was nothing wrong in snatching a little excitement. Was there?

'Sure.'

'Good,' Leo murmured with soft satisfaction. 'It's nice to know that we finally agree on something.'

CHAPTER SEVEN

LEO wasn't sure what demon possessed him. He really hadn't meant to return to his mother's house that evening. Who in his right mind would get in his car in the dead of night to commence a laborious drive into the country, when he could stay in the comfort of his own place which was a stone's throw away from his office?

In fact, he actually returned to his apartment, poured himself a whisky which he didn't drink and then came to the conclusion that for reasons unknown, the cool, undemanding, clutter-free confines of his penthouse apartment, which had been his sanctuary for all these years, now felt inadequate.

At which point he abandoned the untouched drink, switched off the banks of overhead spotlights which cruelly contoured every line and angle of the pale leather-and-chrome furniture and headed for his car.

This was the first time in living memory that Leo had undertaken the trip to his mother's house without first clearing his diary. Under normal circumstances, the visit would be arranged beforehand and he would arrive, usually running late because of work commitments, to a well-ordered and pre-planned weekend. He would undertake his paternal duties, which would involve expensive dining, and the purchase of at least one super-watt gift which Daniel would accept without a great deal of relish. Goodbyes would be said and he would return, with some relief, to the sanity of what he knew best: his work. His apartment. London.

He felt curiously light hearted as the car ate up the miles between London and his mother's house. He was looking forward to the change of environment, he told himself. His makeshift office had worked out even better than he had imagined. It wasn't the clinical, distraction-free zone to which he was accustomed, but it still felt weirdly comfortable.

Then there was Daniel. He had eventually broken through the barrier of his own reluctance and had had the little heart-to-heart chat which Heather had recommended. It had lasted all of fifteen minutes. He had awkwardly reassured his son that Katherine would be back in no time at all, and also that he would be at hand, making sure that everything was all right. Then they had talked about football. In between there had been glimpses of boyish charm, which had made Leo uneasily aware of the truth that life was never as clear cut as you might expect. As he might expect.

Now, cutting through the night, he found himself looking forward to seeing Daniel in the morning. He had managed to get a couple of tickets to a football game in London; prime spot. He figured they might strike a note, which none of his previous presents had, and he was looking forward to seeing his son's face when he was presented with them. With that in mind, he could push back the poisonous surge of regret, which was in a place he knew he was ill advised to visit.

And then there was Heather.

Heather, who would be moving in while Katherine was still in hospital. Heather, who had been at such pains to avoid him, now deciding to set up camp under his roof. Two and

two, in Leo's opinion, made four. Right now, he was playing
with the pleasurable conclusion that, having fought to keep
her attraction at bay to the point where she had knocked him
back with a few snappy remarks about 'being disillusioned'
and 'waiting for the right guy'—who, incidentally, would
never be him—she had finally cracked under the weight of
the inevitable. Namely, she wanted him, and she was now
willing to compromise her principles.

As far as Leo was concerned, it made perfect sense. Her
principles might be laudably high minded, but they were
totally unrealistic. She had talked scathingly of his lack of
interest in emotional involvement, thereby putting herself on
a moral pedestal. Not only would it be satisfying personally
to see her step off that pedestal, he was also doing her a
favour, he reckoned.

She might have been hurt, but hell, what sort of life was
she condemning herself to? Did she imagine that she could
escape all hurt by withdrawing from the process of living? He
was reintroducing her to the notion of involvement: you had
to stick your hands in and get dirty or else what you would
be living was a non-life.

His thoughts were pleasant company for the duration of the
journey which flew past, because at such a late hour there was
little traffic on the roads. By the time he finally arrived at the
house it was very late, but the outside light was on and there
was a welcoming air to the place which, he had to admit, was
lacking in his apartment. There was something to be said for
the crunch of gravel under the wheels of a car, and the soft
murmur of a breeze that didn't carry the sounds of ambu-
lances, police cars and fire engines.

Letting himself in and standing still for a few seconds so
that his eyes could adjust to the darkness, Leo quietly placed

his computer case on the ground and then silently moved towards the curving banister. There was no point turning on all the lights. Heather and Daniel would both be asleep. He might have the kind of constitution that needed very little sleep, but he could appreciate that most people were not built like him, especially children.

By any standards, his mother's house was big. The first floor housed myriad rooms, including a small sitting-room. It had struck Leo, when he had looked over the floor plans from the Estate agency, as very handy for an older person. His mother could watch television at night without having to trek upstairs to get to her bedroom. It was now shrouded in darkness. He was glancing absentmindedly through the half-open door when the blow to his shoulder blades caught him by surprise and had him reeling against the wall. He regained his control and swung round, fists clenched in anticipation of teaching whoever had hit him from behind a lesson they wouldn't forget any time soon.

He knew it was Heather by her height; nothing else could be made out because the corridor was in complete darkness. He reached out and grabbed her hand before the five-inch thick, hardback book could deliver another well-aimed blow.

'What the hell do you think you're doing?'

Between swinging her hand and the book making contact with the intruder—an encyclopaedia of the type now virtually extinct, thanks to the Internet, but still in plentiful supply in Katherine's library—it had clicked in Heather's head that the intruder in question was Leo.

She hadn't had time to pull back from hitting him with cracking accuracy between his shoulder blades, which he was now rubbing with one hand.

She couldn't make out the expression on his face, but she didn't think he would be smiling indulgently at her mistake.

'I'm sorry, but you shouldn't be here!'

'Why are you always so shocked when I show up in my own house?'

'It's not technically *your* house, and you told me that you were going to be away for the night. I…I heard a noise…'

'I tried to be as quiet as possible!'

Heather could feel her heart beating like a drum inside her. Having spent the entire evening thinking about him, to see him now, towering over her, made her feel as though the oxygen was being sucked out of her body. He was like an addiction, and when he was around every ounce of her felt alive. She wondered whether he was aware that she was trembling.

'That's just it…I'm a light sleeper. I heard something, and I assumed it was a burglar.'

'So you just rushed out here, armed with…what is it? One of my mother's books?' Leo felt a rising tide of anger rush through him as he contemplated the consequences of her stupidity, *had* he indeed been a burglar. 'A…let's have a look now.' He relieved her of the book and pushed the light switch on the wall. 'Oh yes; an encyclopaedia of plants. Just the thing you'd need to protect yourself and Daniel against someone who might have been carrying a gun. Or a knife.'

'I'm sorry. I didn't think.' And she wasn't doing too well in the thinking stakes now either. Leo looked neither tired nor crumpled after his long drive out of London. In fact, he looked infuriatingly wide awake and every inch the staggeringly sexy alpha-male that had haunted her thoughts. Realising that she was inappropriately clad in her dressing gown, which she had hurriedly shoved over her shortie pyjamas, Heather pulled the cord tightly around her middle. But even that gesture of modesty couldn't staunch the tingling feeling in her nipples or the dryness in her mouth. She was crazily conscious of his masculinity as he continued to look at her with frowning concentration.

'Well, you damn well should have!'

'Lower your voice! You're going to wake Daniel!'

'I'm not finished with you. We can carry on this conversation downstairs.'

'I'm not coming downstairs with you. I'm tired. I want to get back to my bed.'

'Tough. Follow me.' He spun round on his heels, and after a few seconds of agonised indecision Heather grudgingly followed him down the staircase, still clutching her robe tightly around her as if afraid that it might fly open of its own volition and expose her swollen, tender breasts and stiff, aroused nipples. Her thoughts were everywhere, but she knew that there was no way she would get any sleep that night if she didn't pursue the conversation to its natural conclusion.

Instead of heading to the kitchen, where she expected he might want to make himself a cup of coffee, he peeled away towards one of the three sitting-rooms on the ground floor, and the only one which was actually used.

'You could have been killed,' he told her abruptly, moving to switch on a lamp on one of the many coffee tables before taking up position on the squashy, flowered sofa.

'*You* could have been killed on the way here,' Heather immediately countered. 'You could have lost control of your car and wrapped yourself round a tree.'

'Impossible. Sit. Please.'

'So you *do* remember what I said about not liking being ordered around.' She perched on the side of the sofa, simply because she didn't care for the thought of arguing with him across the width of the room in the early hours of the morning. 'What do you think your mother would have done in my position, if she had heard a noise? And it's happened before, for your information. Okay, it might just have been the house creaking, but she's done exactly what I did.'

'She told you that? She never told me. When did this happen?'

'The last time was several months ago, shortly after Daniel had arrived. She probably would have hunkered down and ignored the creak, but when there's a child in the house hunkering down isn't an option—and, short of sleeping with a gun under the pillow, you just have to use what you've got to hand.'

'I will need to do something about this. Why didn't she mention anything to me? No, scrap that question.'

Heather saw the flash of painful realisation that Katherine had kept quiet because she hadn't wanted to bother her busy son who had no time for her or her life in the country which was so far removed from his.

'It's a big house, Leo,' she said awkwardly. 'And it's old. Big, old houses make noises, and they can be a little creepy at night.'

'I had the most sophisticated alarm-system installed when the house was bought,' Leo pointed out, frowning.

'Katherine doesn't like to switch it on at night. She thinks she might wake up in the middle of the night to get something to drink and set if off by mistake.'

'Right.'

'Also, Daniel might, as well, and he'd be terrified if he set it off.'

'So you prefer to make use of the encyclopaedia of plants instead?'

She knew that he would be having a hard time understanding, probably never having been scared of anything in his life. 'It's pretty heavy.'

'I can't see my mother having the strength to lift it.'

'She probably uses the concise version.'

Leo looked at her and then threw back his dark, arrogant head and laughed. When he stopped laughing, the atmosphere had subtly changed. There was a sudden, charged intimacy in the air between them, and Heather found that she was holding her breath, riveted by his proximity and unable to tear her shamefully hungry eyes away from his face.

'You make me laugh,' Leo admitted roughly. 'Not many people do. I like that.'

Heather felt disproportionately good at that confession. This was what he did to her. He made her feel like a woman and not just like a faceless, sexless person who helped out at charity fund-raisers, pursued her isolated career, tended her garden and helped out at the local school. He made her feel wanton and youthful, and she had forgotten how that felt. Even when she had been married to Brian she had not felt that.

'And you make me feel…' She ran out of steam, and her half-finished sentence hung tantalisingly in the air between them.

'How? How do I make you feel? I'll take a couple of guesses here—angry? Pissed off?'

'That as well.'

'As well as what?'

'I…I should go back to bed.'

'No, you don't. You're not doing a runner on me, Heather,' Leo growled, catching her arm and pulling her back before she could take flight.

Heather gave a little yelp of dismay as she lost her precarious balance and toppled back onto the sofa, half-falling against him, and then stumbling frantically to right herself, in the process coming into way too much contact with his body for her liking.

His body was warm and hard, and feeling it under her

hands sent her mind into a tailspin. She half-closed her eyes and drew in a deep, steadying breath.

No, he wasn't holding on to her. No, he wasn't trying to pin her down or take advantage of her vulnerable position in any way whatsoever. In fact, he was in the process of straightening up so that she could angle her body away from him, but the guilty pleasure she had tried so hard to deny before finally accepting it now exploded inside her like a bomb that had been waiting to detonate. She was shaking like a leaf as she turned her face up to him, and reached forward, closing her eyes and blindly searching out his mouth.

Leo stifled a groan and awkwardly shifted his weight under her, because the erection pressing tight against his zip was downright uncomfortable.

This was what he had wanted, what he had felt assured would be the eventual outcome between them—but now that the moment was here he was compelled to recognise that this wasn't just any woman who would happily hop into bed with him at the snap of his arrogant fingers.

For Heather, this was a very big deal and for once Leo was not inclined to accept what had been handed to him on a plate with the easy presumption of a man who always, but always, got what he wanted.

He gritted his teeth, fighting the savage urge to wrap himself around her soft, womanly body, and instead gently eased her away from him just far enough so that her eyes flickered open and she looked at him in drowsy confusion.

'What's wrong?' Having come this far, Heather was appalled to realise just how much of herself she was willing to commit, and just how ready she was to take the plunge and hang the consequences.

'Nothing's wrong for *me*. I just want to make sure that this is what you want to do. I want to make sure that you're not going to pull away at the last minute and then accuse me of taking advantage of you.'

Heather settled fully against him. She could feel his erection stirring under her. Having long ago come to the conclusion that Leo was not a man who ever flirted with self-denial, she was disconcerted by the way he was looking at her now, his fabulous eyes lazy and questioning.

'Are you…are you trying to tell me that you've had second thoughts?' she asked in a light, shaky voice, and he pulled her down towards him in a kiss of shattering intensity. Heather clung to him, shuddering as his tongue plundered her mouth, tasting the wetness of his tongue and melting faster than an ice cube in a desert.

'I think you can feel what kind of second thoughts I might be having.' Leo pressed himself against her and she groaned when she felt his arousal.

'I think it's safe to say that you've just crossed the point of no return.' He shoved the dressing gown, now tangled around her, off her shoulders while she feverishly untied it from the front, still kissing him and wriggling in her efforts to loose the barrier of clothes between them.

There was something sweetly girlish about her eagerness to touch him, like a kid going wild in a candy shop, and he couldn't get enough of her in this mood. Her soft, full breasts were squashed against his chest, and he pushed up the small vest she was wearing to circle her back with his hands. It was mind-blowingly erotic to know that she was naked against him, that there was no bra working as a potential chastity-belt, in position to save her from herself in the nick of time.

'We should… A bedroom…'

'Is Daniel likely to wander down here at this hour of the

night?' Leo swirled his thumbs against the sensitive sides of her breasts, tickling her with the feathery caress which made it even more difficult for her to think straight.

'No, but it feels odd to be…doing this…*here*.'

'You mean with the family photos looking down at us?' Leo asked drily as he kissed her very slowly and very tenderly on her mouth, breaking off to punctuate his sentence, and then trailed his tongue against her swollen lips; Heather felt that she could have throttled him until he gave her just a little bit more.

'Now that's really done it.' She giggled and looked up to where his father appeared to be benevolently surveying the scene.

'My bedroom, in that case, although it's going to take a hell of a lot for me not to yank you down somewhere on the stairs and have my wicked way.'

'You want me *that* much?'

'Too damn much for my own good. Definitely too damn much to lie here discussing it with you when I could be tearing your clothes off and losing myself in that fabulous body of yours.' The control which Leo had thought he'd brought to the table disappeared fast under her willing submission, which was more of a turn on than he had ever imagined possible. He couldn't quite get his mind round that. Women had always been submissive when it came to him, hadn't they? So why did this feel so special?

They made it to his bedroom, just, tiptoeing past Daniel's room and pausing to hear the slow, steady rhythm of his breathing as he peacefully slept with the door very slightly ajar.

By the time they were in his bedroom, Leo was barely able to contain himself. He shut the door quietly behind them and then pushed her against it, ridding her of her clothes with as much urgency as she was intent on ridding him of his, standing so close to her that the accidental touch of their bodies seemed to generate an unholy heat inside him.

He was shaking as he reached down to cup her breasts, feeling the weight of them in his hands, sending her into orbit as he rubbed the pads of his thumbs over her stiff nipples while simultaneously grazing the side of her neck with his lips. He was desperate to see her, to feast his eyes on her beautiful body, but instinct told him that to switch on the light might frighten the inexperienced Heather off, and there was just no way that he was going to jeopardise what was proving to be the most erotic experience he could remember in a long time. Instead, he led her to his king-sized bed. She was fascinated by his nudity, by his impressive size. He could sense her eyes on his body even though he couldn't make out the expression on her face.

'I haven't, um, done this for a while…' Shorn of her clothing, Heather wrapped her arms protectively around her. She wasn't getting cold feet, far from it, but it was beginning to sink in that she was now in physical competition with all the sophisticated, urban, brainy, impossibly glamorous women he had bedded in the past.

'I like that…' He slowly and deliberately pulled her hands down to her sides and remained holding them, trying to keep his body in check as his eyes did a leisurely and enjoyable tour of her naked body.

Acutely self-conscious now, Heather blushed furiously under his lingering inspection, just thankful that he had been thoughtful enough to keep the lights off, although the curtains in the bedroom had not been drawn, and the silvery moonlight was sufficiently bright for him to clock that she was neither tall, slender or fashionably flat-chested. In fact, she was the opposite.

'You're perfect,' Leo surprised himself by saying, and Heather lifted her eyes to look at him hesitantly.

'Don't tease, Leo. There's no need. I'm not ashamed of how I look or anything like that, but I'm pretty realistic about my body.'

'No, I mean it. You're perfect,' he told her urgently, then, overwhelmed by the impact she was having on him, he backed her towards his bed until she found herself with the soft, downy duvet puffed up around her.

Her eyes had grown accustomed to the semi-darkness and she could easily make out the lean, athletic muscularity of his physique, the perfection with which his broad shoulders tapered down to his waist, the length of his powerful legs. The sight of him made her feel faint and excited at the same time, and the appreciative way he was looking at her revived her flagging self-confidence, introducing a spark of wantonness that she hadn't known she possessed. Where had that come from? Hadn't he told her that he thought she was *perfect*?

Of course, she wasn't a complete fool. She had a very limited time to bask in the accolade, because his attention span when it came to the opposite sex was brief by his own admission, but he had been sincere in the compliment and it had done wonders for any lingering doubts she might have been nurturing.

'So are you,' she murmured boldly as he stepped towards the bed.

Those three small words fired him up in a way no litany of compliments from his other lovers ever had. He lowered himself onto the bed and confessed, shakily, that it was going to be a real challenge to make their love-making last, to give her, without rushing, the most memorable experience she would ever have.

'I'm just so turned on,' he further admitted, straddling her and then sealing any more conversation with his mouth as he kissed her into a state of heated abandon, without so far laying a finger on any other part of her body aside from her face. In the end, she guided his hand to her breast, but he laughed softly in her ear and told her, 'Not yet.

'Ever heard of tantric sex? Shall I show you how sexy words can be? I can get you so close to the edge without touching you that you'd tip over if I just breathed on you. Would you like that? Or are you too hungry for me? Your choice.' He laughed softly, loving her compliance underneath him, knowing that she would have plenty of opportunity to show him her fire. He parted her legs and ran his fingers along the moist crease until she groaned loudly, begging him to take her.

When he had imagined her begging for him he had envisaged feeling a sense of triumph. If he did feel triumphant now, it was lost in the power of his answering emotion, a mixture of hunger, need and uncontrollable craving.

He was beginning to get an idea of what people meant when they said that they just couldn't help themselves. In the past, he had always been contemptuous of any such notion, figuring that when excuses were in short supply that was the inevitable lame fallback. Now he wasn't so sure. He might be in the driving seat but he wasn't too sure if he was steering the car.

'I want you,' Heather breathed huskily. 'And I can't wait.'

'Music to my ears.'

Heather watched with indrawn breath as he kissed his way down and finally paused at her heaving breast where he began ministering to one stiffened nipple, first teasing it with the tip of his tongue until she could bear it no longer, then pressing his head down so that he could take the engorged disc into his mouth, suckling on it while he continued to caress her other breast, leaving her breathless and whimpering and arching up under him so that she could feel the hardness of his erection against her.

It was exquisite torment. He had promised not to rush, and he was true to his word. When she could contain herself no longer, and made to touch the honeyed dampness between her legs that was driving her crazy, he caught her straying hand and responded by hauling himself up into a kneeling position, all the better for her to taste him and feel his big body shudder as she licked and caressed his rigid length.

It was a massive turn on to raise her eyes and see this powerful, unbearably sexy man shorn of his control, his head flung back as she lavished all her attention on pleasuring him.

When he curled his fingers into her hair and pulled her away from him, she knew it was because he was only a whisper away from losing control completely and she stilled as his raspy breathing steadied.

'Bad girl.' He grinned wolfishly down at her. 'Now I'm going to have to punish you…'

The punishment was tactile and verbal as he explored every inch of her restless body, murmuring smouldering, sexy endearments that made her turn to liquid. No one had ever talked dirty to her before, and it was amazing how primitive and erotic it could be. By the time he trailed his tongue along the flat planes of her stomach, Heather felt that the merest whisper of a breath could send her spiralling out of control.

He gave her a few seconds for her body to reach some semblance of calm, before nudging her thighs open with his hand and lowering his head between her legs so that he could breathe in the essence of her.

Heather felt a flare of panic at this shocking act of intimacy. Her experience when it came to men was strictly limited to her ex-husband, who had never had a great deal of interest in the concept of foreplay. She squirmed away from Leo's inquisitive mouth, but he was having none of that.

'I've never…' She stumbled anxiously over her words and he soothingly ran his hand along her thigh. He was incredulous that there were such huge gaps in her sexual knowledge. To have been married and not explored the glory of making love seemed to him a crime, and an indictment of the kind of man she had chosen to hitch her carriage to. If she had been married to *him*…

Closing his mind to a concept that had become totally alien to him after his own bad experience, and disconcerted that he had even been thinking along those lines, Leo resolved to show her just what she had been missing.

She quivered uncontrollably as he parted her womanhood so that he could run the tip of his tongue along her, gently honing in on her most sensitive bud. He felt her draw her breath in sharply as he began teasing it.

It felt unbelievably good to be pleasuring her in this way, giving her the first of what he wanted to be many new experiences. Even this brief flash of life with a woman planned ahead was something to be shoved away. He concentrated on driving her wild, lost himself in her body as she bucked and arched against him, her hands clutching at the duvet as his tongue continued to pleasure her.

He had told her to lie back and enjoy. But at the moment, with his dark head burrowing between her legs and his tongue sending her into rapturous response, lying back was the last thing Heather was capable of doing. Her body was seized by spasms of sheer, sensuous, wanton pleasure. She could hear the blood coursing hotly through her veins, and she had zero control over her own charged limbs as she raised her pelvis to his mouth.

She moaned when she was rocked to an explosive orgasm, and she hadn't even surfaced from that earth shattering experience when Leo drove into her with a grunt of satisfaction, picking up a grinding rhythm that sent her hurtling back to climax for a second time.

She was breathless when they eventually came down from their passionate heights, and was suddenly overcome by a wave of shyness so that she rummaged to draw the duvet around her.

'Bit late for modesty,' Leo murmured wryly. He propped himself up on one elbow and tilted her face so that she was looking at him. What he wanted to ask her was *was that the best sex you've ever had?* And this surprised him, because Leo didn't do insecurity, not on any front and certainly not on the physical front.

'And don't even think of telling me that it was all a mistake and you're never going to come near me again.' He reached over to plant a delicate kiss on her thoroughly ravished lips. 'And don't drape that duvet over you.' He yanked it off and let his eyes boldly roam over her flushed body. 'You have a fantastic body. Curves in all the right places.' He trailed one long finger along her waist and then over her breasts, circling her nipples and laughing softly as the tiny buds tightened under the feathery caress.

'Since when are curves fashionable?'

'You don't really believe that, do you?'

'I guess not.' Heather laughed and then looked at him seriously. She wanted to touch him so badly that it hurt, but she had to have the big 'what happens next?' question answered. 'Although I came pretty close to it when I found out that my beloved husband had been having affairs behind my back. Affairs with very skinny women who didn't embarrass him by doing something so uncool as *eating*.'

'Remind me never to bump into that creep,' Leo said. 'I might be tempted to send him on a one-way trip to Mars courtesy of my fists.'

'That's very gentlemanly of you,' Heather said, astonished, and Leo flushed darkly and shrugged.

'I have no time for married men who fool around. I might play the field, but I have certain codes of conduct, believe it or not.' He rolled over onto his back and stared up at the ceiling.

'Does your code of conduct permit one-night stands?' Heather asked lightly.

Leo turned to look at her. 'Is that your way of asking me whether I want more of you?'

'Maybe you should be asking me whether *I* want more of *you*.'

'You're kidding, right?'

Which was a sharp reminder of just how he saw her, Heather thought. He might wax lyrical about her body, but to him she was an amusing interlude, a break from his normal routine, someone who should be happy and grateful that he had found her attractive. She wasn't going to feel sorry for herself, though. She had made her choice—which didn't mean that she was going to jettison her pride.

'No, I'm not kidding.'

Leo tensed. Had he been thinking *long term*? No. That wasn't his style. Been there, done that. But he had been thinking longer than a night. Having been put in a position where he wasn't calling the shots, he was uneasily aware of a feeling of impotence and he didn't care for it.

'Don't think,' Heather said carefully, 'that because I've slept with you, that I've dumped all my principles about waiting for the right guy...' Some primitive instinct for survival kicked in, making her realise that the last thing she should do was hand over all control to him. 'I haven't, because you were right about not confusing sex with love.'

Leo knew that he should have been relieved at that, but why was his relief taking the form of irritation? Why was he thinking that that just wasn't what he was in the mood to hear?

'Are you trying to tell me that you're just using me for my body?' He could hear the dark edge to the lightly spoken statement.

'It's a very nice body.'

'But you're still waiting for Mr Right.'

'And he's going to show up one day.'

'But, meanwhile, why not give in to a little temptation?' This was all good, he told himself. In fact, it couldn't have been better. 'Suits me.' He cupped her face possessively, stirring into response as her breasts brushed his arm. 'Now, why don't I show you what a long way a little temptation can get a girl?'

CHAPTER EIGHT

HEATHER had had no real idea where she imagined their relationship heading. She had given in to wild impulse, to a driving desire to fling herself into the maelstrom of living with her emotions and not just with her head. That had been two weeks ago and now, as she sat in the quietude of her studio—which Leo had had transported to Katherine's house with breathtaking speed and efficiency—she allowed herself a little time to contemplate the ramifications of her well-intentioned lapse of judgement.

Overall, not that good.

She picked up her paintbrush and began the delicate work of daubing colour onto the meticulously drawn illustration she had been working on for the past few days, but her mind was a million miles away.

She wondered how, in the space of only fifteen days, her harmless little fling had become her all-consuming obsession. Since when could a fling become such a big deal that she couldn't actually see beyond it? Wasn't it actually called a *fling* because it was something passing, something from which the recovery prospect was good—a bit like the common cold? And, that being the case, why was it occupying her every waking moment in what she could only think was a very unhealthy fashion?

She gave up on the illustration and instead swivelled her chair so that she could look out at the peaceful sunlit view through the windows, which had been flung open to allow in the balmy breeze.

With surprising astuteness, Leo had singled out the most appropriate room for her in which to paint. It was in the attic, a small space with a sloping roof and two generously sized ceiling windows, as well as the two long windows now open. The quality of natural light was unbelievable, and Heather had been quietly chuffed at his unerring instinct in sizing up the one place which she would be able to slot into with alarming ease.

In actual fact, she had been quietly chuffed at a surprising number of things in connection with Leo, starting with his choice of studio space for her, and ending with the amount of time he had devoted to being in the country—even though she knew that he probably had a heck of a lot of commitments in London, which he had doubtless put on hold so that he could be around for Daniel.

He had become a regular visitor to the hospital, where his mother was making a good recovery, and hadn't blotted his copybook once with his son.

The debatable upside of all this time spent being the perfect son and father was that he had been around a lot more than she had anticipated. Often, they had breakfast first thing, and then he would shut himself away in his office while she retreated to her studio to paint. Except that the painting was often interrupted by the soft pad of his steps on the stairs, by the feel of his body as he bent to look over her shoulder at whatever she happened to be working on, by the brush of his lips when they inevitably found the curve of her shoulder.

They made love with an insatiable hunger that thrilled and frightened her at the same time.

Under the onslaught of his continual presence, she felt herself becoming deeper and deeper embroiled in a situation that was as far from being a fling as chalk was from cheese.

And now there were further complications which had been thrown into the mixture, complications which she would have to mention to him when he returned from London later that evening.

If things felt a little crazy, then she had no one to blame but herself. She had allowed a situation to develop and now what had been an exciting white-water ride had become a whirlpool which was sucking her down faster and faster. The worst of it was the shocking realisation that she wanted to be sucked under, she *wanted* to give herself totally and completely to him, and she wanted to do that because she had fallen in love with him.

She had blithely ignored all the warning signs which now rose up to stare her accusingly in the face. She had thought nothing of the way he had taken over her thoughts; the way he could make her laugh and relax in his company; the way she was tuned in to his presence before he even entered a room; the way she had found herself waking up in the mornings with a spring in her step and a song in her heart, like a character from a corny romantic movie.

Now, of course, with that missing jigsaw piece firmly in place, she could see just how and why her safe, cosy life had been first undermined and then dismantled. She felt sick at the prospect of picking up all the pieces once he disappeared back to his London life, with its glittering social whirlwind of high-level meetings and chic cocktail parties full of those sophisticated, glamorous power babes with whom he claimed to be bored. At the time, she had been thrilled to bits by that unguarded snippet of information.

Now, she reflected on *why* it had been so easy to be swept away by every small thing he had said. Hijacked by love, she had been pathetically quick to believe what she wanted to believe. He'd told her that the skinny, beautiful barristers bored him, and she'd guiltily translated it into meaning that *she* uniquely captured his attention. He'd told her that she made him laugh, which was rare for any woman, and she'd invested it with a significance which it really didn't have. He hadn't played any mind games with her because he hadn't needed to. She had managed perfectly well on her own in undermining her pragmatic view of what they had.

She spent the rest of the day working on automatic while her mind went wild, freed from the constraints of pretending to herself that she was in control. By the time she sat with Daniel and supervised his prep, fed him and settled him into bed—noticing the way he now asked after his father when a couple of months ago the mere mention of Leo would have been enough to raise a scowl—her head was spinning.

She couldn't remember ever feeling like this, as though she was entering scary, unchartered territory, even when her marriage had been at its lowest and she had realised that she would have to walk away from it.

Daniel had asked her when his father was due to return, to which she had replied vaguely, 'Some time later, maybe around ten or so.' In fact, it was shortly after eight when she heard the slam of the front door from where she was pouring herself a glass of wine in the kitchen while doing her best to get involved in a rather silly television-sitcom.

Leo was still ridding himself of his jacket as he strode into the kitchen. Most unlike him, he had hurried his meeting along, politely declining the usual drink afterwards to celebrate successful completion of a deal, and had spent the entire trip back to his mother's house in the grip of a disconcerting type of eagerness. He had even been tempted to stop en route when he had happened to drive past a particularly charming florist in one of the nearby villages so that he could personally pick out a bunch of flowers for Heather. But he had managed to resist the extraordinary impulse. What the hell did he know about flowers, after all? His secretary usually saw to that type of thing. Except he knew rather more now about horticulture than he ever had before, having listened with amusement as Heather had acquainted him with all the flowers in her back garden, laughing when he'd told her that it was a sorry state of affairs for a woman in her mid-twenties to know the Latin names of plants.

He smiled when he saw her, his eyes roving possessively over her luscious body, and then he smiled some more when he saw the faint tinge of pink flood her cheeks at his hungry appraisal.

But first things first. He poured himself a glass of wine to join her and asked after Daniel.

'Is he asleep yet?' He extracted football tickets from his pocket and dangled them in front of her. 'Ever seen gold dust? I give you these.' With his eyes still trained on her, he placed the gold-dust tickets on the kitchen counter and lazily reached to pull her to him, murmuring into her hair that he had been thinking about her all day.

This, she thought, was how her defences had been so thoroughly overhauled. His softly spoken words and the feel of his body pressed against hers were lethal weapons. She shivered, wanting to break free, but stupidly clung to him with the glass of wine still in her hand.

He removed it from her, placed it next to his on the counter and did what he had been wanting to do since he had left the house at the ungodly hour of five-thirty in the morning. He kissed her with a thoroughness that had her whimpering and cleaving to him, and hating herself for doing both, when firstly she wanted to talk to him and secondly she knew that she was just digging herself deeper into a hole.

But he turned her on! He undid three buttons on her shirt and slid his hand expertly to cover one of her breasts. She made no move to stop him. The air felt as though it was being sucked out of her lungs; it always did the minute he laid a finger on her. She moaned as he began to play with the jutting nub of her nipple. When he licked his finger and returned it to her roused nipple, she could feel the dampness there race to every part of her body, until she felt like a rag doll that had to be propped up for fear of falling.

'The gold dust might have to wait until morning,' she said shakily, edging apart from him. Her breast was still exposed from where he had fished it out of her shirt, the big, pink disc of her nipple gleaming slickly from his wet fingers. She hurriedly did up her buttons and moved to rescue her drink from the counter. 'I wasn't sure what time you were going to be back, so I told him it was better not to wait up.'

'I got here as quickly as I could,' Leo admitted roughly, thinking back to the unholy haste with which he had dispatched his legal team and headed for his car parked in the basement of his vast office in Central London. He took a sip of his wine and shot her one of those wolfish smiles that could make her toes curl. He walked to the kitchen door and quietly closed it. 'Usually, I wrap up a deal with a slap-up meal with the team. Tonight all I could think about was getting back here. Explain that to me, if you will.'

The old Heather, the one that had existed yesterday, would have basked in that lazy, sexual appraisal that had her pulses racing and her heart beating like a hammer inside her. She wouldn't have cared less about explaining anything. She would have strolled over to where he was still standing by the door, watching her with proprietorial hunger. She would have reached up on her tiptoes as she melted against the hard muscularity of his chest, tilted her face to his with her eyes half-closed, and she would have let her body give him whatever answers he wanted to hear.

The new Heather, however, sidled towards the Aga and busied herself concentrating on the pasta sauce which she had earlier prepared for herself, having thought that he would most likely be eating out in London before returning to the country.

'There was no need for you to rush back,' she said indistinctly to the thick Bolognese sauce. 'I mean, I do understand that you have a job to do in London, and that job is going to prevent you from being here a hundred percent of the time. Don't forget, I was married to a workaholic.' She didn't dare turn round, because she knew that her will power would be threatened the minute she saw him standing there, lean, mean and sexy beyond belief. Stirring the sauce was her cowardly way of buying time.

Leo frowned. This was hardly the rapturous response to which he had become accustomed and which he now took as a given. Maybe she was having an off day. He crossed the room, vaguely noticing the way she stiffened, and dismissed that fleeting observation as a trick of the light.

'You were married to a creep,' Leo asserted. He slipped his arms around her and nibbled the side of her neck. She was all creamy curves, and the knowledge of what lay under those clothes was a fierce turn on. When they had first slept together, she had been wildly aroused but still unsure of herself. She was out of practice, she had later confessed, and she had virtually apologised in case she had been a let down. Leo had been touched by that lack of self-confidence. Since then, with all her barriers truly down, she'd been the most passionate, most satisfying, *hottest* lay he had ever had. He couldn't get enough of her. He frequently interrupted his working day so that he could seek her out and lose himself in her voluptuous body. When he wasn't around her, he caught himself looking at his watch and projecting his thoughts to when she would be back in his arms.

Heather didn't reply. Lust fired through her like a raging furnace, and her eyelids fluttered as she leaned back into him and stopped stirring the sauce, thereby losing whatever thread of helpful distraction it had offered her. She heard her own soft moan which caught in her throat as his hands began wandering the length of her body, unbuttoning her shirt to free her bare breasts which hung full and ripe and waiting to be touched. She gave another low moan as he began to caress her. She was barely aware of him easing her away from the Aga so that he could lean against the counter and continue to slowly manipulate her body from behind, notch by exquisite notch, towards a place of no return.

He was whispering into her ear, shredding her ability to think clearly as he began telling her what he wanted to do to her, where he wanted to touch her, how he wanted to touch her. By the time he slipped his hand under her gypsy-cotton skirt, her body was screaming for satisfaction, but he stopped her from turning around so that she could minister to him the way he was ministering to her, and she was too far lost in her own sensual pool to find the energy to resist him. She parted her legs and his fingers found the wet, slippery core of her and began stroking.

Her feverish response was an unstoppable force against which she had no resistance. She arched back, barely able to breathe, and when she eventually came her orgasm seemed to last for ever as she was tipped over the edge with shocking abandon. It seemed ages before she was once again earthbound, then she swivelled round to look at him, her face still flushed and her nipples still stiff and rosy with arousal.

'This wasn't meant to happen,' she said unevenly, and Leo grinned at her.

'Since when?' Instead of taking her right here and right now, he would wait until later when they were in bed. He would savour the moment. 'We're combustible when we're together. I like that.'

'Yes, well…' Her eyes skittered away from his lazy, searching gaze. 'We—we need to talk, Leo.'

Leo frowned. 'Talk? Now? What about?'

Heather could see that talking was probably the last thing he wanted to do.

'There's been a bit of an awkward development.'

'What kind of awkward development?' Alert to the nuances in her tone of voice, Leo was instantly on his guard as he rapidly sourced in his head what *awkward development* she might want to discuss with him. 'Do I need to sit down for this?' he asked abruptly. He didn't like the way she was looking at him with that cautious, shuttered expression. He didn't like finding that he had driven like a maniac to get here only to find his expectations of the evening going so drastically off-course. It struck him with unpleasant force just how much he had become accustomed to a certain pattern of behaviour between them, and how much he had come to enjoy that pattern.

For a man who had tried the whole domesticity thing and found it wanting, had fashioned a personal life that managed to escape the debilitating tedium of routine and the unacceptable consequences of commitment, Leo was unnerved to acknowledge how much routine had seeped into his relationship with Heather.

He couldn't pinpoint when that had happened. He just knew that he enjoyed having her available for him, enjoyed the smile that lit up her face every time he looked at her.

'If you like.' Heather shrugged. Now that sex was off the menu, she could tell that he wasn't best pleased. Wasn't it the driving force behind their relationship, as far as he was concerned? That *combustible* passion that flared up whenever they were around each other?

He refilled his glass with wine and headed towards the sitting room. Already one thought was forming in his head, a suspicion which took shape and was fully developed by the time she closed the sitting room door quietly behind them.

'Tell me.' He walked towards the bay window and stared outside for a few seconds before turning round to face her. 'That there hasn't been a mistake.'

'Mistake?'

'Don't play dumb with me, Heather,' Leo intoned rawly. 'You know what I'm talking about. We were careful all of the time.'

'*Most* of the time,' Heather corrected. She could see now where his mind was going, and the horror that would be unleashed should she tell him that she had accidentally fallen pregnant. Leo wasn't in it for the long haul, and if she had ever needed proof positive of that fact then she had it now. She felt as though she was being sliced open, but she remained outwardly calm. 'But I'm not pregnant, so you can breathe a sigh of relief.'

Having envisaged the worst, Leo was left oddly deflated by her denial. 'Good,' he said flatly. 'Then what is it?'

'I went to visit your mother in hospital today,' Heather

said slowly. 'She's spotted that there's something going on between us. She's been skirting round the subject the last couple of times I've been to see her, asking me what I thought of you, but today she asked outright.'

'And you told her…what?'

'I really did try to change the subject, but she wouldn't let it go, and in the end I may have mentioned that…that we've become involved over the past couple of weeks.'

'And that's a problem because…?'

'Because she believes that it's more serious than it is.' Heather thought it wise not to mention the extended conversation she had had, during which Katherine had poured her heart out about her misgivings over Leo's first wife, about the rift Sophia had driven between the brothers, a rift that had already been in the making. She had told her all sorts of personal stuff—regrets she harboured that her eldest son had somehow grown to feel shut out over time from the family unit, which he had seen as indulging his younger brother, while from a young age failing to acknowledge the achievements of the older. Her misguided faith that the *relationship* between Leo and Heather, the wonderful changes she had seen in him, would signal a new beginning for Leo had had Heather scuttling out of the room, appalled at Katherine's deductions.

'Of course she doesn't,' Leo denied dismissively. 'You're reading way too much into the whole thing. And, now that that's out of the way, why don't we pick up where we left off in the kitchen?' He moved towards her and Heather looked back at him with stubborn determination.

'You weren't there, Leo.'

'I don't need to have been. My mother has always known, since my marriage collapsed, that long-term relationships aren't my thing.'

'She's a romantic. She's clung to the notion that you've just been in search of the right woman. She said that Sophia wasn't right for you and that you've just been waiting to open yourself up.'

'To *you*?'

'I'm only repeating what Katherine said.' She could feel tears sting the back of her eyes.

Leo instantly recognised his mistake. He could see the hurt spread across her face, even though she made an effort to hide it, and an apology formed on his lips. But he remained silent because just the thought that other people might be playing around with notions of permanence on his behalf was an error he needed to correct. He had no intention of remarrying. If he hadn't said so outright to his mother, then he had always assumed that she had got the message, or why else would he have spent all these years happily playing the field?

He wondered uneasily whether Heather was right, whether his mother had been storing up misguided ideas about him waiting to find 'the right woman'. What was it with women and their pointless belief that a perfectly satisfactory life wasn't possible unless there was some kind of soulmate hovering in the background?

'So what do you suggest?' he asked heavily. 'And stop standing there by the door! You're making me feel uncomfortable.'

'Well, we can't have that, can we?' Heather said acidly, but she took up position on one of the chairs. 'I don't know what to suggest, except that we can't carry on deceiving Katherine.'

'We're deceiving no one!'

'Maybe *you* don't see it that way, but *I* do.'

'So, in other words, we either break things off right now or else we…what? Get engaged? Start looking for wedding rings?' Just when he had got used to having her around, he could sense her gearing up to take flight. Again. What was it about this woman?

'Of course not,' Heather muttered. She harboured a warming image of Leo asking her to marry him. For her, he was her one and only love. The situation into which she had drifted with Brian had been based on what other people had expected of them. This was the real deal.

'You'd like that, wouldn't you?' Leo said softly, narrowing his eyes on her pinkened cheeks. Something was telling him to back away from this conversation; he ignored it.

'I…I don't know what you're talking about,' Heather stammered as the ground threatened to open up under her feet.

'It would have been easy to laugh off Katherine's romantic notions. You could have shrugged your shoulders and told her that we were just having a bit of fun, nothing serious. My mother might well want to see me welded to *the right woman*, and I wouldn't know about that because she's never mentioned that to me, but she wasn't born yesterday.' Leo paused. 'I don't imagine she would be shocked at the reality that a man and a woman, sharing the same house, might have been attracted to one another, might have initiated a relationship. But maybe you didn't *want* to bring her up to speed with the truth. Did it suit you to let her think that there was something serious going on between us?'

'No!' Had it? Had she been unable to conceal her starry-eyed response to Katherine's scrutiny? She had tumbled like a blindfolded idiot into love with Leo, and had his mother spotted that even before she herself had?

'Are you sure about that, Heather?' He was very slowly coming to terms with the inescapable truth that she had invested a great deal more into their relationship than she had cared to let on. He had originally thought that their mutual physical attraction was just too powerful for her to resist, had forced her down from her moral high-ground and ambushed all the goody-goody principles she had been so keen to spout when they had met. She had mouthed assurances that it was all about the physical attraction because he wasn't her type, and, since that had made perfect sense to a man who was physical deep down to the core, he hadn't stopped to question the apparent ease with which she had embarked on their affair.

Now, of course, he knew that she was not a woman to whom sex was the be all and end all of a relationship. Her principles were deeply ingrained in her, and only now was it dawning on him that she had fallen in love with him.

He should be running scared. This was the very last thing he wanted. Indeed, in the aftermath of his failed marriage, he had made a determined effort never to find himself in a situation such as this. He wasn't scared—in fact, he felt weirdly pleased—but common sense put an immediate stop to that feeling.

'I'm not up for grabs,' he said in a cool, matter-of-fact voice. Leo could remember having this conversation before. There had been the occasional woman who had wanted more than he was prepared to give, and he had had to do the let-down speech, although by the time that had happened he had felt nothing. Frankly, by then, he had usually seen the signs of over-dependency and had dealt with the inevitable with a certain amount of relief. Not so now, although he wasn't going to analyse that, because the net result was the same. He was shot through with bitter regret that he would have to forgo the splendours of her body. He was ashamed to admit to himself that he wasn't ready.

Heather was mortified. 'I know that,' she said quickly.

'Do you?'

'Of course I do!'

'Then why did you allow yourself to fall for me?'

Heather sought divine inspiration, but the ground refused to comply by opening up and swallowing her. Had she been that transparent? Humiliation spread through every part of her. She knew that her face was bright red, a sure giveaway that he had hit the jackpot with his remark.

'You're wrong,' she whispered, looking everywhere but at him, although it was pointless, because she could feel those amazing eyes boring straight through her.

'You knew the rules of the game.'

'The game? *The game?* Since when is a relationship a *game?*'

'You know what I mean, Heather.'

'I didn't see it as *a game.*'

'But you *did* tell me that you were in it for the sex. If I recall, you didn't think that we had anything in common except, of course, lust.'

At this point, Heather was faced with two options. The easy one would be to agree. To strenuously deny all his accusations, to somehow manoeuvre a strategic backtrack and just enjoy the very little remaining time that they had together. Katherine was due out of hospital at the weekend. It would signal Leo's return to London, and why shouldn't she just have her fill of him before he headed back down south? Why should she be held captive by her emotions? Okay, he had guessed the truth, had guessed that she was a lot more involved than she had let on. But just because she had admitted that what they had hadn't been a game to her, didn't necessarily mean that she was looking for love and marriage. At least, not if she talked her way out of his assumption.

When she looked at her future without Leo, all she could see was a gaping, black void. Wasn't a couple of days of happiness worth it? She would be picking up pieces for the rest of her life, so why start now when she had the choice of putting it off just for a little while longer? Was she a masochist? Did self-denial win medals for anyone?

'I did think that,' Heather told him quietly. 'At the time. I mean, when we first…when I… Well, I thought it was all about physical attraction, but then I got to know you.' It was getting tricky, looking everywhere but at him, and eventually Heather raised her eyes to his face. His expression was still, shuttered. She knew that this would be a nightmare for him but she wasn't going to skirt round the truth because it was easy. If he didn't like what she was about to say, then tough.

'Or maybe,' she continued thoughtfully, 'I was just kidding myself. Maybe I felt that pull towards you even before I realised—before I realised that I had feelings for you.' She smiled weakly. Even in her discomfort, she was agonisingly aware of his potency, of that strong, masculine pull that emanated from him in dangerous waves. It made her feel giddy, breathless and horribly, horribly weak. She had to draw in a deep, steadying breath before she could continue in the face of his stony silence.

Leo bitterly regretted having brought the subject up. Frankly, he hadn't expected her to confirm his suspicions. Any other woman would have taken refuge in denial, making sure that the way was clear for a dignified exit. Not so this woman— but hadn't he already come to the conclusion that she was a one off?

Unfortunately, the more she said, the faster she would bury what they had. Did he want it buried? Strangely, no. Not that he wanted commitment. He just didn't want things to finish quite yet, and he was hellishly annoyed that she was the one doing the finishing. Role reversals and learning curves were two things he considered pointless in so far as they pertained to him personally.

He raised his hand to stop her mid-flow.

'There's no need to do the whole psychoanalysis thing,' he interrupted, pacing the room, his brows knitted into a frown as he tried to marshall his thoughts. Not for the first time in her company, they were proving strangely rebellious.

'Yes, there is. For me, at any rate.' Mortified as she was, Heather was determined to stand her ground and speak her mind. Things left unsaid meant that closure was never achieved, and besides, why shouldn't life be a little uncomfortable for him? Why should she slink away with a phoney smile and pretend that her heart wasn't breaking?

'Why?' Leo stole a scowling, frustrated glance at her and raked his fingers through his hair.

'Because I like honesty? Because I'm not going to pretend that I haven't fallen for you? I have.' She looked at him defiantly. 'I know it doesn't suit you to hear me say that, but it's the truth. I haven't told Katherine that, so you needn't worry on that score. In fact, I didn't encourage her to think that there was anything serious between us, despite what you said. I know this isn't what you bargained for, but believe me it isn't what I bargained for either.'

She stood up and began edging towards the door. 'I also know that it makes things a little uncomfortable between us at the moment, so I'm going to transfer back to my place tomorrow. You'll have to stay here with Daniel until your mother returns.' She collided with the door and paused, licking her lips nervously, willing him to say something instead of maintaining a silence from which she could deduce nothing whatsoever. Maybe, though, his continuing silence was preferable to his mockery or contempt.

Looking at her as she backed towards the door, Leo had been overcome with an angry, urgent need to stop her in her tracks. The inevitability of this outcome hit him like a sledge-hammer. He didn't know what he wanted to say, but he damn well wasn't going to remain in tongue-tied silence. But before he could utter a word she was holding up her hand. The other hand had already turned the door handle.

'I don't want you to say anything. We both knew that this was going to end, anyway, for whatever reason.' There was a silence that lasted only a heartbeat. 'But, before I go, I mustn't forget to tell you: your brother's coming home. He'll be here on Saturday. In time for when Katherine arrives back from the hospital.' It was good to have the conversation back onto a prosaic level. It helped her diminishing self-control and reminded her that this wasn't some great romantic drama, just an everyday story of two people who weren't destined to be together. He would move on and she would too, eventually.

'Goodbye, Leo.'

She fled. He could hear her retreating footsteps, and he knew that she wasn't heading back up to her room because he heard the slam of the front door. It was as final as a full stop at the end of a sentence.

CHAPTER NINE

HEATHER looked at her reflection in the mirror. She could feel the flutter of nerves in her stomach and it was making her feel sick. Was she wearing the right thing? Was she giving off the correct message? What exactly *was* that message anyway? Some could argue that, having declared your love to a man who had a stone for a heart, there was no appropriate message that could be achieved with an outfit.

She had spent the past three days unable to eat, concentrate or do much of anything apart from think, and her thoughts had been very poor company. She had barely glanced at her work, which she had stolen back from Katherine's house, furtively having made sure that Leo was nowhere around when she had been inside the house. She had, however, checked her mobile phone every other second, or so it seemed, and had wished against the odds that she would hear the distinctive beeping sound of a text message from him. When they had been together he had often texted her, and she still blushed when she remembered the content of some of his messages. But she had not heard a word from him and, while that was precisely what she had expected, the pain of missing him was still unbearable. She had got the closure she had wanted, except it had done nothing to put her on the path to recovery.

And now she was about to see him again—when she still felt raw, bruised and vulnerable.

Katherine had returned from hospital—in fine fettle, although still unable to walk without the aid of crutches—and with the help of Marjorie, the lady who came in to clean the house during the week, she was hosting a dinner in celebration of her son returning from foreign shores.

Heather knew all this because she had been invited to the little dinner party, which was going to be a cosy affair. Just family. And Heather. No amount of helpful suggestions along the lines of, 'Wouldn't it be nice to have some time with your sons on your own? To catch up?' had managed to rescue her from the horror of having to face Leo again.

Which brought her right back to her outfit: casual. Nothing that would indicate that she might, in any way whatsoever, be attempting to attract him: a pair of grey trousers and a black tee shirt with a simple black cotton jacket flung over it, and some plain, black flat shoes. No one, she decided, could accuse her of wanting to draw attention to herself when she was dressed in the most background colours known to mankind. Colours that, coincidentally, were great for bolstering her confidence, because they made her feel utterly sexless. All she needed was the addition of a briefcase, and she might have been going for a job interview at a bank.

Not that she felt in any way confident as she left her house fifteen minutes later. In fact, she felt about as confident as a prisoner being led to the guillotine. She had decided to walk and, the closer she got to the big house, the slower her pace became until she was standing in the cool early evening, staring at the house in front of her, searching out the little attic window from which she had looked down, only days ago, to a breathtaking view of open fields and sky. Leo's car, the gleaming, silver Bentley, was parked at an angle in the large, gravelled courtyard, as was a small, red runabout which Heather knew belonged to the housekeeper who had come for the evening to prepare the meal and do the dishes. Close to the front door was a black motorcycle which looked as though it had seen better times.

Heather took a deep breath and forced herself on with the cheering thought that the evening wouldn't last for ever. In fact, she was determined to stay for as little time as humanly and politely possible.

Also on the plus side was the fact that they wouldn't be alone together. Alex, Katherine and Daniel would all be there as well, and chances were high that Leo would barely notice her presence at all.

In all events, he wasn't there when she entered the house. Where was he?

'He had to rush off to London this morning,' Katherine said, smiling from the sofa where she was sitting with a drink in her hand. 'He hasn't even had the opportunity to see his brother again!' Which drew Heather's eyes to the man sitting next to Katherine—no doubt the owner of the battered motorcycle parked askew outside the house.

Alex had the same set of features as his brother, but without the sharp edges, and with none of the power and arrogance that stamped the contours of Leo's face, giving it its own distinctive brand of sexual potency. When he stood up smiling to shake her hand, she could see that he was a little shorter than Leo and with the wiry body of a cyclist. He didn't threaten her in any way at all and Heather liked him immediately on sight.

Without Leo around her anxiety faded, and as introductions

were made and a drink pressed into her hand she felt herself begin to relax. If Leo had gone to London, then it was unlikely that he would be returning any time soon. She didn't have to be on the lookout. She could give herself over to listening to Katherine and Alex as they chatted animatedly with one another, Alex telling them about his travels, and Katherine chastising him gently about the risks he took living rough on the other side of the world.

Daniel's eyes were like saucers as Alex regaled them with tales of high adventure, teasing his mother that as soon as she was back on her feet she would have to ride pillion with him when he next took off.

'Although,' he mused as they went in for dinner, an informal meal served in the kitchen, 'being here, I kinda think that it might be time to find me a steady wife and settle down…'

'Just what I wish your brother would do.' Katherine sighed, taking her place at a table which had been optimistically set for five. Leo's empty space spoke volumes for his absence. Now that his mother had returned, he had clearly returned to his bad old ways of putting work first, Heather thought.

She noticed that, at the mention of Leo, Alex's face became closed, but the impression lasted only a second then he was back to smiling and joking, involving Daniel in the conversation with a warmth and ease that brought a smile to Heather's face—although, as the spectator watching the mother-son interplay, she couldn't help but feel a strong pull of sympathy for Leo. He had from a young age felt locked out of the family unit, Katherine had confided, felt less loved than his brother and less appreciated for his efforts.

'What he couldn't have understood,' Katherine had told her thoughtfully at the hospital when they had had their heart to heart, 'was that Alex had always just needed more looking after. He never seemed to really know himself the way Leo did. He had always needed reassurance.'

Now she thought about Leo and the way he had pulled back over the years from his family until now, when Daniel and then Katherine's fall had brought him back into the fold. Not entirely, but life, after all, was a gradual process of growing and learning.

She felt momentarily faint, thinking how much she would have loved to be by his side over the years, learning and growing alongside him. Instead, not only had he disappeared but no one seemed entirely sure when he would return.

'You must be really disappointed.' She turned to Alex when there was a lull in the conversation over dinner. 'Having travelled all the way over here to find that Leo's been called away on business.'

Next to her, Daniel was all ears as he demanded to know the gory bits of his grandmother's operation: 'What do you think it looked like, all that blood and stuff? Couldn't you have asked them to take a picture?' All those pressing questions which he had obviously felt constrained not to ask when Katherine had been in hospital, and which Katherine was now strenuously trying to evade, although Heather could tell from the expression on her face that she was close to laughing.

'Leo's always being "called away on business",' Alex told her in a low voice. 'It's his modus operandi. Haven't you noticed? The fact that I have turned up here like a bad penny would have sent him running for cover even faster than usual.'

'But why?' On one side, Katherine was now trying to divert Daniel away from the intricacies of hospital procedure and towards the more harmless topic of the dessert which had been placed in front of him, but Daniel was as stubborn as his father and was having none of it. In a minute he would be off to bed, and he was determined to make hay while the sun shone.

'Call it his way of showing brotherly love,' Alex murmured bitterly.

'Well, this is none of my business,' Heather told him, closing her fork and spoon on her dessert.

'Isn't it? I thought… Mum said that…'

Heather felt her face flame with unbidden colour, but her voice remained steady as she shrugged and gave a little laugh of dismissal. 'Oh, *that*,' she whispered in a shifty voice. *What on earth had Katherine said?* Okay, so it didn't take a genius to hazard a pretty good guess. Leo had clearly said nothing to his mother about recent events, and Katherine still believed that Heather and her son were an item. There had been no opportunity to talk to her, and when Heather thought about the awkward conversation that lay ahead—because she knew that she would have to disabuse Katherine of her romantic daydreams sooner rather than later—she felt a little nauseous.

'That…was nothing.' She gave a nervous, tinkling laugh and took refuge in a large mouthful of dessert.

'Now now, no need to be coy. I think we've known each other long enough for complete honesty. Mum's said Cupid's been busy with his little arrows.'

'You're awful!' But she was laughing, although she could feel the hysteria of tears welling up just below the surface. Thankfully she was spared any further embarrassment by Katherine standing up and excusing herself.

'Daniel needs to go to bed now,' she said, ignoring her grandson's pleas that it was the weekend, that he wanted to see his dad, that no one in his class went to bed before ten on a weekend. 'And I'm feeling rather tired,' she admitted, clasping Daniel's hand affectionately. 'Now,' she said, turning to Daniel, 'are you going to be the perfect gentleman and help an old lady up the stairs?'

'Mum, I'll walk you up.' Alex was already on his feet, but was being waved down by Katherine, who wanted the young things to enjoy getting to know one another.

'I'm just sorry that Leo couldn't be here, but he'll be back home first thing in the morning.' She looked at Heather warmly. 'There's an awful lot for him to return to.'

Heather smiled wanly. She could feel a thin veil of perspiration break out, but this was not the right time for revelations, not when Katherine looked all in and Daniel was yawning and coming over to wrap his thin arms around her for a hug. Furthermore, she thought, why should she be the one to break it to Katherine that the hot item had turned into a damp squib? Hadn't she been put through the wringer enough?

She would stay for a quick cup of coffee with Alex and then she would retreat and leave it to Leo to fill his mother in. After all, she thought bitterly, when it came to letting women down his experience was second to none.

'So tell me everything,' were Alex's first words as they sat on the sofa in the sitting room, he with a glass of port—because, he had told her, travelling the world had deprived him of that one small pleasure—and she with a cup of coffee which she cradled in her hands.

'Shall we start with age?' Heather sipped her coffee. 'Height? Vital statistics? Occupation?'

'All very interesting, of course, but I'm thinking more along the lines of you and Leo. What's going on there? Mum's over the moon. She thinks he's a changed person and it's all down to you. Actually, she's all but bought the hat.'

Heather groaned and sat back. 'I don't want to talk about Leo.'

'Yes, you do.'

'Why,' she asked, half-exasperated, half-amused at his persistence, 'are you and your brother just so damned *stubborn*?'

'You mean I have something in common with Leo?'

'You don't have an awful lot of time for him, do you?'

Alex wagged an admonishing finger. 'Uh-uh. No way. You're not getting off that lightly.'

Heather compressed her lips and stared down at the sensible black pumps which in all events had been an unnecessary gesture. Leo hadn't even bothered to turn up. He'd been that horrified at her admission that avoidance had been his chosen way of dealing with the prospect of seeing her again.

'How long are you here for?'

'Another attempt to change the subject. Things must be bad. 'Course, if you really don't want to talk about it then I'm happy to chat about your occupation, but it's always better to get things off your chest. Or else you risk ending up like Leo.'

It wasn't so much his tenacity as the sympathy in Alex's voice that did it. The tears that had been threatening like black clouds on a summer day came in a sobbing rush that frightened her with its intensity. She hunched over on the sofa and buried her head in her arms. When she felt Alex's arms enfold her, she turned to him blindly, thankful for his silent, accepting compassion. For the past few days she had kept her feelings locked up inside her, and now it was a relief to have someone else share the burden.

When she felt the handkerchief thrust into her hand she grabbed it gratefully, and after a while the racking sobs subsided to the odd hiccup until she was able to draw back and make an attempt to gather herself.

Unburdening herself of her feelings about Leo was like shedding herself of a great weight, and once she had started the need to tell everything was an unstoppable force, helped by the fact that Alex was an excellent listener. There were very few interruptions. As her words trailed off into silence, he told her that she needed a brandy, and she nodded in agreement even though she had never touched brandy in her life before.

He was still holding her hand. Every so often, he patted it sympathetically. His voice was a low murmur, which was very soothing, although she wasn't really taking in a word he was saying. She was back to thinking about Leo, thinking about the love she had confessed to, wondering what he was doing right now. Would work keep him away all night or would he be filling the space she had left behind with another woman? Just the thought of that made her clutch at the handkerchief again.

Neither of them noticed the figure in the doorway. The overhead light hadn't been switched on, and the light from the small lamp on the table by the mantelpiece barely managed to reach the far corners of the room.

The sound of Leo's voice, ice-cold and forbidding, shocked them into springing apart. Heather felt the blood rush to her face and she stared helplessly at him. His face was in shadow, but there was no mistaking the angry tension of his stance.

'Am I interrupting something?'

Alex was the first to react, leaping to his feet with a grin on his face, but Leo stayed where he was, making no effort to move forward and take the hand which was outstretched towards his in a gesture of welcome.

'I was about to leave,' Heather muttered, lagging behind with the response. She was finding it hard to drag her eyes away from Leo's face. She was mesmerised by the long lines of his muscular body, the same body which had covered hers in love-making. She looked at his mouth, the same mouth which could do things to her that no man ever had, and overwhelmed as she was she still couldn't stop her body from its purely physical response at all that remembered passion. Her nipples tightened into sensitive buds and she felt hot moisture dampen her underwear.

'We were just getting to know one another.' Alex's hand had dropped and he was eyeing his brother cautiously—as well he might, Heather thought, because Leo looked fit to kill. She felt a slow, burning anger begin to curl in the pit of her stomach.

Leo might have done his best to avoid her, might be enraged that she was still hanging around when he thought that the coast was clear, but that didn't give him the right to vent his anger on his brother.

'What exactly were the pair of you up to?' Leo asked in the kind of soft, sibilant voice that sent a tremor of apprehension racing up and down her spine.

'*Up to?*' Alex countered the preposterous question with a laugh, but Heather could hear the nervousness behind the laughter and her heart went out to him because when it came to everything there was no contest between the brothers: physically, verbally… Leo would always be the winner and right now, for reasons she couldn't understand, he looked very much as though there could be no better thing than taking on his brother.

'Leo! What on earth are you talking about?' Heather made to move towards him, but fell back at the glance he shot in her direction.

What am I talking about? The innocence of the question was like a red rag to a bull. 'I'm talking about finding the two of you huddled on the sofa like love birds,' he bit out, taking a step towards her, although what he really, really wanted to do was cover the distance between himself and Alex and show him who was the boss. Respect for his mother kept him from fulfilling the desire, but if he kept his fists clenched to his sides this was still a war that had been a long time coming.

'Leo, please,' Heather pleaded in growing confusion. Was he jealous? Those were the enraged, possessive remarks of a jealous lover, but since when had Leo been either possessive or jealous? There was also something else going on here. The air felt thick and heavy with threat.

'*Love birds?* You must be joking, Leo! I told you, Heather and I were just talking.'

'About what? What conversation is so intimate that it requires you to be entwined with one another?'

'We weren't *entwined*,' Heather protested, while her heart continued to beat out an erratic tattoo.

They had leapt apart like guilty lovers, Leo thought irrationally, and the more they defended themselves the more culpable they seemed to him. Rage was coursing through him like a toxin. He didn't know where it was coming from. He could almost taste it in his mouth, and he had to breathe deeply to regain some of his formidable self-control.

Was it his imagination or did she look ever so slightly tousled? This was the woman who three days ago had confessed her love for him, shocking him with her honesty. He had felt as though a gauntlet had been laid down, and it had not been one which he had been inclined to take up. He had never given her the slightest inclination that there could be a future between them. Not only had she chosen to disregard that glaring point of truth, but she had stubbornly refused the two options which had been left open to her—either slink away with a discreet lack of fuss, or else put aside her silly dreams and continue their relationship, which would have been his preferred path. She must have known, he had told himself repeatedly, that to fling all her cards on the table would put him in an untenable position.

He was a man who was not fashioned for long-term relationships. Hadn't he made that perfectly clear to her during the time they had spent together? More than with any previous woman, he had actually opened up to her under direct questioning, and had told her certain things about his marriage which had previously been kept in his own private terrain. Of course, he had not told her everything, but combined with everything else— and no one could say that he hadn't been upfront from the start—the least she could have done was take the hint.

Women, the very few who had ever dared to nurture inappropriate ambitions as far as he was concerned, always but always took the hint.

He had spent three days telling himself that he had to be ruthless when it came to this one woman who had dared to crash through the barriers he had carefully, over time, constructed around himself.

He had decided that he would have one final conversation with her, clear the air.

The last thing he had expected was to walk in on her and his brother cuddled up on his mother's sofa in virtual darkness.

Thinking about that now, Leo banged on the lights and proceeded to look first at her and then at his brother.

'I didn't think you would be back tonight.' Heather filled the awkward silence with the worst choice of explanation and the taut lines of Leo's face darkened further.

He hadn't expected to find her still at the house, and this was the last thing he needed to hear. Was this how she was managing to deal with her unrequited love? He was besieged by a host of unpleasant, conflicting emotions. He had never before been aware that he was a man who had a comfort zone, a place which was inaccessible to the rest of the human race. He was now keenly aware that she had managed to barge right into it, because he didn't feel himself, and it wasn't because his brother was back on the scene.

Leo found that when he tried to think about it his brain seemed to shut down, leaving him floundering in a morass of weirdly unanswerable questions. He didn't like it. It distracted him from the purity of his rage, forced him to ask *why* exactly he was so enraged. Was it just the thought that she might have declared her love for him—and she hadn't been lying about that, because hadn't he been the one who had sensed it, probably even before she had herself?—only to find herself in thrall to his brother, of all people?

'Where did you think I would be?'

'Katherine said that you had gone to London. It's so late; I thought you might have stayed there overnight.' Even with his face stony cold and her emotions all over the place, Heather was vitally aware of that leashed power and grace that was so hypnotic. His impact on her was so powerful that it made her feel giddy. 'I…I should leave. You and your brother probably have a lot of catching up to do.'

In his mind's eye, Leo was tormented by the picture of them sitting together in a darkened room, so close to one another that you couldn't have put a cushion between them. Normally adept at eliminating anything that threatened to disturb his much-valued equilibrium, he was finding it impossible to erase the distasteful memory from his head.

He made himself look at Alex. By active choice, he had only seen him a handful of times over the years and it struck him that, yes, his brother was a man who might seem to him lightweight but to some women could easily appear appealing. He looked vaguely unruly, just the sort to ride his battered motorbike around the world. Just the sort to be on Heather's wavelength. A free spirit. His tension ratcheted up a notch and a sense of purpose crystallised inside him like a block of ice.

'Yes,' Leo agreed, unsmiling. 'But, first, let me apologise

for misunderstanding a situation.' He turned to Heather and forced himself to smile. 'You'll have to excuse a lover for being a little jealous.'

Lover? Wasn't *ex-lover* a more fitting description of their current status? She looked at him in total bewilderment. *Jealous?* She would have been more capable of appreciating that startling sentiment if she wasn't presently feeling as though she had somehow been transported to a parallel universe.

'But—but—' she stammered in utter confusion as he began walking slowly towards her. She glanced across to Alex, who seemed as perplexed as she was, and then back to Leo.

So she had confided all in his brother. Leo caught that exchanged glance, and at once read the situation as it really was. She had been pouring her heart out to Alex. The jealous rage that had swept over him had been misplaced. She loved *him*. The certainty of that knowledge, while frustrating—because he could have spared himself his momentary lapse in self-control—was surprisingly soothing. For once he didn't mind being wrong about a situation.

'A lover's tiff,' he threw at his brother while moving to curl his long fingers in Heather's hair. It felt good. Better than he would have imagined possible. It also felt right, which was odd, considering he had spent three days building up a strong case for talking to her without the interference of emotions about where exactly she had gone wrong in trying to pin him down.

He felt himself harden, and it was an effort to bring himself down from that sudden surge of hot arousal. It was her proximity, the tempting fullness of her half-opened mouth.

Unable to resist, he lowered his head and took her mouth with his. 'You've been crying,' he murmured against her lips. 'Was it because of me?'

'Leo, no...' Heather pushed him, but she was trembling so

hard and he was an immovable force. He caught her fluttering hands in his and repeated his softly spoken question, demanding an answer, and when she gave an imperceptible nod he was momentarily overwhelmed by a surge of pure, primitive triumph.

Heather couldn't bring herself to meet his eyes, but she could sense his satisfaction at her miserable, grudging surrender, and she pulled back angrily. She forgot that Alex was still in the room. Leo could do that to her, make her forget everything, and he was doing it now. For what? To prove that he *could*? He didn't love her and he didn't want her, but maybe he just didn't care for the thought of her wanting someone else. He was a man who had become accustomed to absolute and supreme control. His high-octane, hugely successful financial acumen had won him an army of yes men, and his ludicrously powerful sex appeal had enabled him to snap his fingers and have any woman sprinting in his direction. So now that same desire to control would doubtless dictate that she pine for him.

She glared up at his arrogantly smug face and stamped down on her body's weak, automatic response to his proximity. She was shaking as she wrenched herself away from him.

'I fell for you, Leo,' she told him, keeping her voice low, controlled and steady. 'And, sure, right now I'm a little down in the dumps. But I won't be crying for you for the rest of my life. I've already cried over one failed relationship.'

'Don't even *think* of putting me in the same bracket as your ex! I've already told you that the man was a creep!'

'We were too young when we married, and he was weak. Since when are *you* any different?'

'I'm a one-woman man,' Leo responded comfortably, still riding high on the notion that she had been crying over him.

Of course, he abhorred the thought of her being unhappy—but being unhappy on his behalf was a hell of a lot better than flinging herself into someone else's arms as a method of recovery. 'I don't play the field when I know that there's a woman keeping my bed warm for me.'

'You're a one-woman man for just as long as it suits you,' Heather flung back at him, taking another step backwards and folding her arms. 'You talk a lot about making sure never to give a woman the wrong idea, but I think you quite enjoy the thought that you can get them into a position where they'd do anything for you. 'Course, that gets boring after a while, but when you walk away you can always remind them that you never promised them anything.'

'That's called being *fair*.'

'That's called being *a creep*. You're just a different kind of creep, Leo!'

Leo flushed darkly, outraged at having had what he considered to be his impeccably fair reputation dragged down into the dirt in the matter of a single sentence. Against his better judgement, he began to rapidly revise his satisfied acceptance that what he had confronted in the sitting room was a distraught Heather offloading on his no-good brother. What if she had already been subconsciously comparing him to Alex? Was Alex a creep? No. To her, he would have seemed as wholesome as freshly baked bread with his 'let's hold hands and discuss our feelings' approach.

Jealousy and possessiveness, two weaknesses he had always prided himself on not having, rose in him like a red mist. To top it all off, his brother at that very instant had the barefaced cheek to tell him, 'Perhaps you should take time out and, hey, maybe listen to what someone else has to say for a change?'

'And maybe *you* should listen, little brother. She's off-limits.'

'Hello?' Heather interjected furiously at Leo's ferocious verbal warning to his brother. 'Are you talking about *me*? Because, if you are, I just want to remind you that I'm not your *property*, Leo!'

'You're in love with me!'

Heather fell silent, cursing the one, wild moment in time when she had been drawn to be honest with him. Now, he was using her love against her. Tears of hurt and betrayal stung the back of her eyes, and she looked down at her feet, willing herself to fight against the temptation to really let the side down by crying. Once, in front of Alex, had been quite enough.

And I'm not about to let you go. That thought sliced through Leo's consciousness like a razor blade, shearing away at his fundamental acceptance that the chosen path of his life was to remain free of the encumbrance of a woman tied to him by a band of gold. He had his son. It was enough. He was not even aware that he had spoken his thoughts out loud until Heather, standing as still as a statue, asked him to repeat what he had said.

'You're right,' he told her, walking towards where she had managed to field him off by edging towards the mantelpiece. He was no longer aware of his brother. It was as if a genie in a lamp had magically made him disappear. There was a roaring in his ears, but still he felt good. Calm. 'I'm a different kind of creep.'

'Wha...?' The whole parallel-universe thing was happening again. She wanted to move out of Leo's reach, but her feet stubbornly refused to oblige. What had he been talking about when he had said that he refused to let her go? Had she heard correctly? Her heart was beating so fast that she felt faint. Or maybe it was just the way he was staring at her, his fabulous eyes reaching down into the depths of her and stirring everything around. It was so unfair that this was what love was all about: allowing someone in who had the power to scramble your brains.

'I am prepared to make a commitment to you,' Leo announced with largesse.

'You're "prepared to make a commitment" to me?'

'Correct,' Leo asserted.

'What sort of commitment?' Heather asked faintly.

'Are there different kinds?' He frowned, just a tiny bit thrown by her lack of a suitably rapturous response.

'Yes, there are different kinds!' Heather was compelled to point out, because her mind, which had turned to cotton wool for a moment, was finally cranking back into gear and warning her that their definitions of commitment would almost certainly not coincide. Leo's idea of commitment would be, in his opinion, to generously allocate a few months rather than a few weeks to a relationship, and to maybe tone down the tenor of his remarks when discussing any plans that stretched beyond a two-day time limit. Accept that, her mind was telling her, and she would be no better off than she was now. In fact, she'd be worse off, because she would have longer to fall even deeper in love with him.

'How so?' Leo demanded, but cautiously.

'You know how I feel about relationships,' Heather told him quietly.

'Then maybe,' he said in an undertone, 'we should get married.' He was gratified by the alteration in her expression. After everything he had been through over the past few days, he had never expected to land up in this place, and from the look of it neither had she. It was as if suddenly he was released to have her, and any misgivings about finding himself in such wildly unexpected terrain were wiped out by the knowledge that she was now his.

Predictably, he felt his body harden as his imagination ran amok, conjuring up pleasurable images of exploring her naked body, tasting her, losing himself in her fabulous curves. His eyes smouldered in anticipation of touching her, but for the moment he interrupted her stupefied, gaping silence to say quietly, 'I'll leave you to think about it, hmm?' He reached out and curled a finger into her hair, and admitted what he had been so strenuously denying for days—that, yes, she took his breath away. 'Because now there are things that have to be said between my brother and me.'

Think about it? Heather was in a daze. She felt as though, if she probed too deeply into his extravagant proposal—which seemed so out of keeping with everything she had assumed about him—then it would disappear like dew on a hot summer day.

'But—'

'No *buts*.' He kissed her parted mouth, a kiss that was both chaste and deeply, deeply sexy at the same time.

'Okay.' Heather sighed when his lips finally left hers.

'And we'll talk…later.'

Afterwards, a mere three hours that felt like three decades, Heather wondered what that promised land would have looked like had fate not decided to show her, had not guided her foolish steps back to that sitting room with two mugs of coffee to find that the door was ajar, just a slither. Just enough for her to overhear a conversation that was as destructive as a hammer shattering a pane of glass.

Sitting in her cottage while the clock chimed midnight she wished she could cry, but she was all cried out for the moment—although she suspected that, when the tears finally came, they would never stop. She would just drown in her own self-made misery.

CHAPTER TEN

THE past three hours had been cathartic for Leo. Indeed, he felt as though he had been sucked into a whirlpool, spun around at dangerous speed and then spat out. He had been stripped of his cynicism; of course it would return in time, because that was part and parcel of his personality, but right at the moment he felt weirdly exposed.

He also still had to talk to Heather. He was looking forward to it. In fact, he couldn't wait.

Having become accustomed to her being under the same roof as him, it was only when he was virtually outside the door to the room she had used while she had been in his mother's house that it struck Leo that she wouldn't be there. She naturally had returned to her cottage. He spun round on his heels and took the stairs two at a time, leaving the house as quietly as he could and choosing to walk to her place, giving himself a head start on collating his thoughts.

Although it was after two in the morning, he didn't feel in the least tired. In fact, he felt fantastically alive, and filled with a driving sense of purpose. Although it made more sense to wait until morning, because she would probably be fast asleep at this hour, Leo felt compelled to see her as soon as was physically possible. He didn't doubt for a single second that she would feel exactly the same way about seeing him.

As expected, her cottage was in complete darkness, but he didn't hesitate to ring the doorbell, and was slightly surprised, although pleasantly so, when she answered the door within minutes. Nor did she look as though she had been dragged out of bed. In fact, she looked as alert as he felt, which was great.

Leo grinned and stepped forward. 'I didn't wake you, did I?'

Wake her? Not much chance of that when she had spent hours replaying in her mind those stolen snippets of revealing conversation which she had overheard before she had fled. No, she had had no more chance of sleeping with so much on her mind than if Daniel had set up camp in her bedroom to play his drums.

Besides, it seemed a moot point whether he had woken her or not, because he was already inserting himself beyond the door, shouldering his way into the cottage.

Heather cravenly wished that he would just disappear, leaving her some more time to sort out in her head what she was going to say to him. When fate decided to play games, she thought, heart beating a frantic tempo, it certainly didn't cut corners. Leo was the opposite of the disappearing man— he was standing in her hallway, one hundred percent vital, insanely sexy male.

'I'm glad you came.' Heather found her voice and made it sound as cool as possible, although her fingers were knotted nervously behind her back as she watched him remove his weather-beaten, tan leather bomber-jacket and sling it over the banister.

In the cold light of reality, she had taken time to consider his extraordinary marriage proposal. It had been the last thing she had expected, and she was ashamed now at how eagerly she had allowed herself to believe that he had really meant it.

Leo had never once talked to her about a future, not even when their relationship had been at its rosiest. In fact, he had been positively scathing about such a concept applied to him and any woman. Nor had he given her any inclination, when she had told him about his mother's assumptions—when she had *confessed her love*—that he was willing to commit to what they had and give it a fair go to see where it ended up. No, he had been more than willing to walk off into the sunset, leaving her to deal with her broken heart.

She was retrospectively incredulous that she had succumbed to his phoney, soft voice and honeyed words and had actually believed that he had come to some kind of wondrous realisation. She couldn't now comprehend how she had been so stupid. The man didn't love her, never had and never would. Really, how on earth could he have come to a wondrous conclusion that he had made a mistake, that he wanted her in his life? Even when he had uttered that preposterous proposal he had significantly failed to say anything about love. She had let herself believe what she'd wanted to believe, and it wouldn't be the first time she had made that particular mistake around him.

'We need to talk,' she told him in a stilted voice, solving the problem of looking at him by turning her back and walking towards her sitting room. She waited as he followed her in, but when he sat down, patting the space next to him, she remained standing by the door until he finally caught her mood and frowned.

'You are upset because I should have come sooner,' he said as an apology. 'There were things that needed to be said between my brother and myself.'

'Yes. I know.' Heather swallowed hard. She was so alive to his presence that it hurt. It was like being high up on a mountain where the air was thin and breathing normally was impossible. It was not how she wanted to feel, not now, and she had to make a big effort to keep her voice level and her thoughts as clear as possible.

'Sometimes,' he carried on, 'family situations can take longer than anticipated.'

'Yes. I know.'

'Is that all you're going to say? And why are you standing all the way over there by the door when there's a much more comfortable spot right here next to me?' *Where you belong*, was the unvoiced postscript to that remark, and incredibly he didn't try and rail against it.

'I've been thinking about what you said, Leo—about marriage—and it doesn't make any sense.'

Leo's deep, grey eyes, which could be as cold as slate when he was angry and as dark as coal when he was aroused, swept over her cautiously.

'You see,' Heather continued, pushing herself away from the door and sidling sideways, crablike, to collapse onto the chair facing him. 'I happened to overhear a bit of what you and Alex were talking about.'

'How is that possible?'

'I came back; I thought the two of you might want some coffee. The door was open and I heard…stuff.' The 'stuff' had become a jumble of words that had crystallised into a lethally destructive bomb threatening to explode in her head.

'Stuff that made me realise that you don't give a jot about me,' Heather told him. She was hanging on to her self-control, but only by a thread, and if he couldn't hear the angry tremor in her voice then *she* certainly could. 'You didn't ask me to marry you because you had decided that you wanted to build a future with me. You asked me to marry you because Alex was in the room and you felt the need to exercise your rights over a possession. Because there's a lot of muddy water under your bridge, isn't there, Leo? Would you ever have told me if I hadn't found out on my own?'

'You should not have stood out there listening to a conversation that was private!' Even as the words left his mouth, Leo was chillingly aware that there were more holes in that line of argument than a colander. Of course she would have listened, probably caught by the mention of her name, or maybe just by the urgency of their voices. She was only human. He felt out of control, and he didn't like it, but then again when had he felt completely in control since he had met her? He could no longer remember that happy state, nor did he have any inclination to return to it.

'That's not the point. The point is…' She heard the wobble in her voice and took a deep breath. 'I was just a bit player in a revenge game for you, Leo.' Big, fat tears were welling up and she swallowed hard.

'You're getting hysterical.'

'I am *not* getting hysterical!'

'No? Because your voice is getting higher and higher. Why don't you let me explain?' A lifetime of self-control made it possible for Leo to outwardly contain all nuance of emotion in his voice, but already he was considering the possibility that one overheard conversation would be the conclusive nail in his coffin, and a thread of panic was beginning to filter in. He wanted to go over to her, close the distance between them, but he knew instinctively that the result would be either fight or flight, and neither was acceptable.

'Explain what?' Heather asked him jerkily. 'How it is that you let your ex-wife destroy the relationship you had with your brother? With your son?'

The silence stretched between them, thick and tense. Heather wondered whether he would say anything. He was a deeply private man, and having her raise the spectre of a past he probably would have preferred to keep under wraps, she half-figured, would make him simply stand up and walk away.

Leo heard the scathing, incredulous criticism in her voice and for the first time in his life he found himself lost for words. The very basic foundation of his life—which was that essentially he didn't much care one way or another what someone else might think of him—deserted him.

'What you overheard has nothing to do with you.'

'How can you say that?' Heather asked. She stared at the man sitting opposite her and wondered who he was. There was no expression on his face. He wasn't going to explain anything to her because she just didn't *matter* enough. Since when should that thought hurt her? she wondered. It wasn't as though it came as any blinding surprise.

Since when had she ever really mattered to him? Even when he had been covering her body with kisses, touching her in her most intimate places, tasting her in ways that could send her into orbit, he had never let the barriers down. He lived life the way people might play a game of chess, always coolly conscious of needing to make just the right move. Wasn't that why he was so phenomenally successful in business? Leo did nothing unless it suited him. At that particular point in time, it had suited him to make a big song and dance of claiming her in the most irrefutable way he could think of.

'Alex and I were having a private conversation,' Leo said heavily. 'And one that was perhaps overdue.'

'*Perhaps?*'

'Sophia destroyed many things, and I allowed it.' For someone as open and as upfront as she was, she would find these dark secrets abhorrent. But he needed to explain before he could even begin to find out whether he had missed his chance with her, as he knew he probably had. 'I never questioned what she expected out of me, but I knew very early on that I was failing to deliver—too much time spent at work, not enough interest in going out to clubs or partying. My wife, in short, discovered that the man she married wasn't the fun-loving guy she wanted. It escaped her that I needed to work in order to earn the vast sums of money she enjoyed spending.'

'You don't have to tell me any of this if you don't want to,' Heather said. She was painfully aware that the words were wrenched out of him. While he maybe thought that the very least she deserved was clarification from *his* point of view, of things that had been said, she still shied away from causing him any discomfort. She could feel her tender heart reaching out to him.

Leo looked briefly at her and then vaulted to his feet so that he could pace the small room, a tiger forced to withdraw its claws and leash its primitive urge to dominate. Which made her no less conscious of his immense, restless energy. Even in thoughtful contemplation he still managed to overwhelm his surroundings and make her acutely aware of her fascinated response to his physical impact.

In that single sentence—*you don't have to tell me any of this if you don't want to*—Leo thought that he could identify her retreat from him. Why else would she show such little interest in a story that was so revealingly intimate? He hadn't thought that he had loved her. Hell, who knew what love was? His experiences in that field had been blighted, to say the least. How was he supposed to know, belatedly, that this powerful urge to be with her, the way she had filled his head, had been more than just a passing inconvenience? He had never had a problem compartmentalising women before. How was he supposed to recognise that his inability to do the same with this woman was an indication of feelings that were as alien to him as breathing air was to a fish?

He gave an elegant, casual shrug in the hope that it would conceal his desperation to make her understand.

'I don't pretend to have been a saint. I was away more often than I should have been, but returning to the house was like returning to a hell hole. Even after Daniel was born the arguments continued. In fact, they became worse, because added to the general gripe that I didn't pay her the attention she deserved was her resentment at being housebound. Even with nannies at her disposal her freedom of movement was curtailed, by her standards, and she didn't like it.'

Having heard only the bare skeleton of her eavesdropped conversation, Heather was silent at this unexpected fleshing out of the detail.

'Well?' Leo prompted, because her silence was unnerving. She was a woman who had opinions on just about everything, up to and including things which were outside the boundaries which he had silently but firmly laid down between them.

Heather looked at this clever, complicated, beautiful man who had stolen her heart without even trying, and she did her best not to be utterly transparent.

'Was that when she…um…?'

'Decided that an absentee husband wasn't good enough? Realised that infidelity was just the thing? Began screwing around?' Leo gave a short, humourless laugh. 'No idea. The end result was the same, and thrown into that wonderful hotpot was Daniel. She was determined that I not get close to him. I don't think she could stand the thought that there reached a point when I just didn't really give a damn about her any longer. I wanted my son, but as far as I was concerned she could have disappeared off the face of the earth. When I told her that I wanted a divorce, she went crazy, and she went even crazier when I didn't react.'

Heather had no difficulty in imagining the scenario. Leo, at the height of his indifference, was a formidable sight. She shivered. Was this story just a prelude to telling her why he had asked her to marry him? She could feel herself clinging to the miserable hope that he must care something for her if he was going to all this trouble, divulging details he had probably never shared with anyone else in his life before. She firmly squashed the feeling.

'You know what happened next, don't you?' Leo was finally standing in front of her, a towering presence that sucked the breath out of her. Heather nodded slowly, because 'what happened next' had been the very first words she had accidentally overheard. Leo dragged the small, upholstered footstool across so that he could perch on it. A big, brawny, muscular man on a dainty pink footstool—it was a comical sight, but the last thing Heather felt like doing was laughing.

Giving in to feelings of sympathy that were beyond her control, she reached out and rested her hand lightly on his shoulder, although it seemed an inadequate way of expressing her compassion. Which, it struck her, he may or may not even want.

How else could she let him know that she was appalled at the wickedness that had motivated his ex-wife to take Daniel to the furthest reaches of the universe, and not before she had constructed her cleverly woven lie that the child wasn't Leo's?

'She was evil, Leo. I realise you probably don't want to

hear this cliché but the past is over and done with, and today and tomorrow are all that matter.'

'Sometimes clichés can be very helpful.' He looked directly at her, and as their eyes tangled she felt her breathing sharpen into staccato bursts; typically, she thought, ambushing the cool demeanour she was so intent on portraying. 'It's unforgiveable that I have waited this long to confront my brother, but then that was probably what motivated Sofia to tell me that Alex was Daniel's father. She knew that it was the one thing I would find impossible to deal with, although I carried on attempting to maintain contact. Three times I made elaborate attempts to visit, and three times Sofia made sure that she went AWOL with Daniel. Then came the pictures of her and Alex, supposedly playing happy families behind my back.'

He released one long sigh, closed his eyes and swept his fingers through his hair. 'History now. Alex was there all right. He was in Australia, passing through, apparently, on one of his many "let's see as much of the world as I can" escapades, and he managed to corner her to find out what the hell was going on. At which point she played for the sympathy vote and implied all manner of things.'

'I'm…I'm really glad that you sorted everything out with your brother, Leo.' In fact, whilst it had taken time for him to warm to his son, big bridges had been built, and they had a relationship which she suspected would only get stronger and stronger.

She made to pull her hand away but Leo prevented her from doing so, placing his on top, a warm, heavy weight that made her pulses race. In a minute, Heather thought that he might pat her gently on her arm and give her a fond, brotherly peck on the cheek before sending her on her way.

'But I still think it was pretty inconsiderate of you to stick me in the middle of your argument. I guess when you were still of the mind that he had slept with your ex-wife that was just your way of telling him that he wasn't about to take what was yours again—but, hey, I was *never* yours.'

'That's not the impression you gave me a few days ago when you told me that you—'

'I don't want to talk about that!' Heather looked away, her cheeks flaming under his searching, narrowed eyes.

'Why not?'

'Because…'

'Because confession, you now realise, is not necessarily good for the soul? Because you've finally realised that love is an overrated option that comes with too many unpleasant side-effects? Because you've met Alex and realised that the world is full of more suitable candidates?'

'What does Alex have to do with anything?'

Leo's mouth tightened. He stood up, his body language speaking volumes for his tension. He wasn't sure how to manoeuvre the conversation to a place that felt more comfortable. He had just told her things which he would never have repeated to another woman in a million years, but how was she supposed to know that? In her world, people were honest and open and didn't have secrets that they kept to themselves for years on end, allowing lives to be damaged.

'I am nothing like my brother.' Leo shoved his hands into his trouser pockets and scowled darkly at the ground as he paced the floor. 'Alex has always been the *sensitive* one.' It was a description which, over the years, Leo had fine-tuned into an insult. Now, he was beginning to see the positives behind it.

'Some guys are,' Heather said softly.

'And no doubt you find that very endearing.' He paused to shoot her a frown.

'Are you *jealous*…?'

'I'm not the jealous type,' Leo grated, but dull colour slashed his high cheekbones. 'Did he try anything on when he was busy listening to you and providing a handy shoulder to cry on? No, scratch that question. I never asked it.'

'You *are* jealous!' Heather breathed, hardly daring to explore that wonderful concept too hard just in case it shattered under scrutiny.

Leo sat back down, because pacing up and down was making him feel even more like a caged animal, and decided to bite the bullet.

'I have a problem thinking of you with another man,' he admitted in a driven undertone.

'Why?'

'Why do you think?'

Heather struggled to find a suitable answer to that demanding question, but the drag of her senses to the man now staring down at her was wreaking havoc with her thought processes.

'Some people, some *men*, have a dog-in-the-manger attitude towards women,' she ventured uncertainly. 'Even if they don't want a woman, they don't want anyone else to have her.'

'That theory doesn't just apply to men. Anyway, you're wrong.'

'Why, then?'

'I didn't ask you to marry me because I wanted to assert proprietorial rights over you.' Leo side-stepped the direct question in favour of taking a more leisurely path to what he needed to say. For once, the preferred direct route with which he was accustomed to dealing with everything and everyone was not working for him.

'Why, then?' She was no longer trying to squash that little bud of hope that had taken root and was squirming steadily upwards.

Between them, the silence vibrated. Leo flexed his fingers and looked down at them before raising his eyes to her face.

'I never thought that I would love a woman. I'd been through hell on earth with Sofia, and as far as I was concerned commitment was for the birds. When you told me that you loved me, I didn't stop to think. I just assumed that it wasn't on the cards. Only…' He thought back to the way she had continued to prey on his mind, the way he had thought up excuses for contacting her again, the way he had subconsciously never contemplated a future without seeing her in it somewhere.

Heather was holding her breath.

'When I saw you there on the sofa, I saw red. I didn't stop to think, and even when I did I still couldn't stand the thought of you being in a two-metre distance of Alex. I figured that he was more your type than me.'

'He's a sweet guy, but he's not *you*, Leo. I didn't want to fall in love with you but I did, and there's no way I could ever fall out of love with you, no matter who else comes along.'

'No one else is going to come along,' Leo told her, locking his eyes to hers with fierce possession. 'Will you marry me, Heather? As soon as possible? Tomorrow?'

Heather laughed, light-headed with happiness, and she flung her arms around his neck and pulled him to her. This was one dream she was not going to be letting go of any time soon…

'As soon as possible' turned out to be four months. It would have been cruel, she gently told Leo, to deny Katherine the chance of really enjoying the day, not to mention Daniel, and of course Alex, who had decided at long last to put down roots. *Literally* roots, as he was in the process of opening a garden centre just outside the village with the help of his mother and, naturally, Leo, whose financial acumen would be essential to its success, he had asserted the minute the idea had first been broached.

Their wedding had been a quiet affair and afterwards had come the process of moving. Although thankfully, as far as Heather was concerned, not to London but to a village slightly more accessible for road and rail links and not very far away from Katherine so that Daniel could continue at his school.

Heather hadn't believed Leo when he had told her that he was a changed man, that his workaholic days were over, but he was true to his word, and only left the country when absolutely necessary. She felt blessed to be on his learning curve with him as he forged deep bonds with his son, finding shared interests in the most unlikely places.

And now…

She looked at the kitchen clock and her heart gave its familiar little lurch as she heard the click of the front door opening. When he walked into the kitchen, bringing with him that wonderful scent that was so peculiarly him, she walked straight up to him and curved into his open arms. Two whole nights away from him because he had had to go to New York to close a deal. Nearly three nights, when you worked out that it was almost ten in the evening.

'Next time you're coming with me,' he growled, smothering her in kisses, feeling as though he was finally coming home where he belonged as her body pressed against his. He tenderly unbuttoned her shirt and sighed with gratification as he saw that she wasn't wearing a bra.

'Don't you want to eat first?' Heather breathed, blissfully happy when he said that he had other things on his mind to eat that had nothing to do with food. The passing of time had not diminished their craving for one another, and their bodies were so finely tuned to each other's needs that his light touch against her thigh had her parting her legs, offering every inch of her body for his exploring hands.

'No panties,' he murmured into her ear. 'Just the way I like it…' He had long ceased to marvel that every time he touched her he felt as aroused as if he were touching her for the first time. Sometimes they could not even make it to the bedroom, and tonight was one of those times.

'You and Daniel,' he said with raw honesty, 'are the lynch-pins of my entire life.'

'And soon you'll have another…' The news which she had been hugging to herself for the past day brought a radiant smile to her lips. 'I'm pregnant.'

A new life beginning, a new journey, and there was no one in the whole world she would rather share both with.

Coming Next Month

in **Harlequin Presents®**. Available July 27, 2010.

HPECNM0710

HARLEQUIN®

A *Romance*

FOR EVERY MOOD™

Spotlight on

— Heart & Home —

Heartwarming romances
where love can happen
right when you least expect it.

See the next page to enjoy a sneak peek
from Harlequin® American Romance®,
a Heart and Home series.

Five hunky Texas single fathers—five stories from Cathy Gillen Thacker's LONE STAR DADS *miniseries. Here's an excerpt from the latest,* THE MOMMY PROPOSAL *from Harlequin American Romance.*

"I hear you work miracles," Nate Hutchinson drawled. Brooke Mitchell had just stepped into his lavishly appointed office in downtown Fort Worth, Texas.

"Sometimes, I do." Brooke smiled and took the sexy financier's hand in hers, shook it briefly.

"Good." Nate looked her straight in the eye. "Because I'm in need of a home makeover—fast. The son of an old friend is coming to live with me."

She was still tingling from the feel of his warm palm. "Temporarily or permanently?"

"If all goes according to plan, I'll adopt Landry by summer's end."

Brooke had heard the founder of Nate Hutchinson Financial Services was eligible, wealthy and generous to a fault. She hadn't known he was in the market for a family, but she supposed she shouldn't be surprised. But Brooke had figured a man as successful and handsome as Nate would want one the old-fashioned way. *Not that this was any of her business...*

"So what's the child like?" she asked crisply, trying not to think how the marine-blue of Nate's dress shirt deepened the hue of his eyes.

"I don't know." Nate took a seat behind his massive antique mahogany desk. He relaxed against the smooth leather of the chair. "I've never met him."

"Yet you've invited this kid to live with you permanently?"

"It's complicated. But I'm sure it's going to be fine."

Obviously Nate Hutchinson knew as little about teenage

boys as he did about decorating. But that wasn't her problem. Finding a way to do the assignment without getting the least bit emotionally involved was.

Find out how a young boy brings Nate and Brooke together in THE MOMMY PROPOSAL, coming August 2010 from Harlequin American Romance.

Brides

*A powerful dynasty,
eight daughters in disgrace...*

Absolute scandal has rocked the core of the infamous
Balfour family. The glittering, gorgeous daughters are in
disgrace.... Banished from the Balfour mansion, they're
sent to the boldest, most magnificent men
to be wedded, bedded...and tamed!

And so begins a scandalous saga of dazzling glamour
and passionate surrender.

8 volumes to collect and treasure!